If the Heart Is Lean

YELLOW SHOE FICTION

Michael Griffith, Series Editor

If the Heart Is Lean

stories

MARGARET LUONGO

Luong

Louisiana State University Press)|(Baton Rouge

NATIONAL
ENDOWMENT
FOR THE ARTS   This publication is supported in part by an award
from the National Endowment for the Arts.

Published by Louisiana State University Press

Manufactured in the United States of America

LSU PRESS PAPERBACK ORIGINAL
FIRST PRINTING

DESIGNER: Barbara Neely Bourgoyne
TYPEFACE: Myriad Pro, display; Warnock Pro, text
PRINTER AND BINDER: Thomson-Shore, Inc.

Library of Congress Cataloging-in-Publication Data

Luongo, Margaret, 1967–
    If the heart is lean : stories / Margaret Luongo.
       p. cm.
    ISBN 978-0-8071-3376-7 (pbk. : alk. paper)
    I. Title.
    PS3612.U66I5 2009
    813'.6—dc22
                            2008010719

The paper in this book meets the guidelines for permanence
and durability of the Committee on Production Guidelines
for Book Longevity of the Council on Library Resources. ∞

For Billy Simms

and my family

Contents

If the Heart Is Lean

Pretty

I love being drunk. Is that bad? Barhopping downtown with the people from work, everything seems good and possible. As we walk from our first bar to our next, it seems possible I could love my job; it seems possible I could someday have a career. Love for my coworkers seems plausible, too. Love radiates from my breastbone for Stan, the bearded senior editor with baggy wool trousers and starched white shirts. The sympathy I feel for Elaine, who wears a Dorothy Hamill haircut twenty-plus years after it was fashionable, brings tears to my eyes. I lust for Julius, the deep-brown stringer who is gay. He wears ankle-high black leather boots with his purple and orange suits. I'm staring at him and he catches me, winks. I wink back and reach behind Elaine as we walk, trying to pinch his arm. His arm is hard from workouts at the gym. I could maybe love Lynette, my office mate, if she were here. If she didn't work so hard and so late, it would be much easier to like her.

We pass a café where people like us have dinner after work. The outdoor tables are full of well-dressed men and women, eating small salads by candlelight. I fall behind the group and stare openly at a man in a shirt so white it glows in the dimming light. His tan is deep and fake, but I love him for it. I imagine taking hold of one of his big arms and giving him a bite. The woman he's with notices me staring.

I wrinkle my nose at her, wave, and run to catch up to Julius and the rest of the group.

We turn the corner and pass my bar—The Town Hall—the one I go to by myself. I look through the window as we pass, trying to see who's there. It's the usual bartender, and some of the regulars.

We stop at Earl's to shoot pool. We'll keep drinking there. Julius orders us cosmopolitans. Elaine drinks white wine spritzers, Stan, Irish beer. The bar is full of people escaping the numbness of their air-conditioned offices. I check out the groups at the bar—the men in their suits, the fit ones who look like *Vs*, the dumpier men with ill-fitting trousers. I love them all, and if they would look my way they could see that. Some do and I smile, nod. My smiles and nods will yield nothing; I know that, but I'm drunk and my consciousness is blurred and I'm not patient enough to wait for the rest of the bar to catch up.

A couple of skinny white guys shoot pool beside us. The one closer to me wears a denim jacket over his jeans and black t-shirt. Pinned to his jacket are rows and rows of buttons, like colorful armor. From this distance I can't read them. He has full lips and thick brown hair. When he bends to take his shot, a lock falls forward, nearly touching the tip of his nose. He parts his lips, and I wonder about their softness. I walk up to him, bend slightly, and read aloud the sayings on the buttons.

"Question Authority," I read. "Kill Your TV."

He doesn't acknowledge me; I keep reading.

"The Sinn Fein are watching." I tap it with my finger, the nail clicking. "What's that about?"

He still doesn't look at me. He keeps his eyes on the game. "It's about death," he says. "It's about manipulation."

"Oh," I say, backing up slowly. Some people don't want to be happy.

Julius is there when I turn around. He hands me my red drink. We toast each other.

"To handsome men in purple suits," I say.

"To bony white girls with big tits," he says.

We drink. I decide to stick with my colleagues for the rest of the evening. The button guy has shaken my confidence. To prove I'm having fun, I smile too hard and laugh too loud. I laugh at Jules's jokes and Stan's jokes; I slap their arms and lean in close. Elaine doesn't participate, only looks at me in that tired, knowing way of hers. At one point, I'm sitting on Jules's lap, trying to get him to describe his bedroom to me. He's laughing and blushing. Stan howls. Elaine pushes her chair away from the table and walks to the bar for another drink. Later, I slip off to the bathroom during a long story of Stan's when I realize I can't pretend any longer to be interested. I look grim in the mirror, in here without an audience. Without the forced cheer, the smiles, the eye-crinkles, I look like an inmate. I've seen their arrest pictures in the newspapers. That impossible tiredness, the gaze that doesn't bother to look out but isn't looking in either. Unfocused, I'm thinking, when Elaine comes in.

"What's up?" I say, not feeling any need to smile for her. She knows something, probably more than I do. She's in her forties and tries to give me advice, but most of the time I don't understand what she's trying to tell me and I just get annoyed.

"Not much." She washes her hands at the sink after I've moved away. "I'm heading home. Need a ride?"

Normally I would prefer to ride home with Stan or Jules. Stan gives me little kisses and squeezes before I get out of the car—drunken affection he's smart enough not to pursue; he is my boss, after all, and he'd have to face me at work. I wouldn't mind, but I bet he would. Jules and I chat cattily about people we've seen at Earl's. Tonight, I imagine we would talk about Button Guy. I'm not up for it.

On the way to her car, Elaine tells me about a job opening at a new food magazine. "I know the managing editor," she says. "I could get you an interview."

I haven't mentioned that I'm looking for a job because I'm not. "Huh," I say. "Sounds interesting."

"They want someone young for restaurant reviews. You know, where the up-and-coming of the professional world hang out. The go-getters of your generation. The office is in Dupont. It's a younger crowd. Hip." She smiles at me. "I've seen the first issue—it's high-end. I'd go, but I'm too old."

"I doubt I'm hip enough," I say, trying to be funny, trying to downplay that I am in no way a go-getter.

Elaine gives me a cool look. "They want a good writer with a young person's perspective. That's you. It would be good for your career."

I start at the word "career." I don't often think of myself in conjunction with that word.

"When are they hiring?"

"Now. Fax your résumé tomorrow. I'll look at it for you."

"I don't think I can get it ready that fast," I say. I wonder why Elaine's pushing so hard.

"I'll tell my friend you're on deadline, but you'll have a résumé to her by the end of the week."

Her tone says, Don't fuck this up. I'm handing it to you.

"Thanks, I'll do it," I say, because I want her to stop talking.

At work the next morning it's hard to get going. I drink a Coke from the can, through a straw. The stockings do not feel good. They make my feet sweat, but we have to wear them. A map of the United States covers my desk. I'm proofreading it. I never realized how many states have towns named "Jefferson." Some have more than one. Normally, on a morning such as this I would nap hard, facedown on my desk. I would take an early lunch and return ready to crank on my projects. When I'm motivated, I can get twice as much done as most people in the same time. Now, however, I share my office with Lynette, a thirty-five-year-old single mother, an entry-level editorial assistant. Gone are the days of midmorning naps, or any naps at all, for that matter.

I try to forget she's there, but it's impossible. Lynette brings with her an air of heaviness. It's partly her age that depresses me, combined with her shitty station in life. I graduated from college last year at twenty-one and I had her job. Partly, too, it's her clothes. Her clothes are old, not just unfashionable, though they are unfathomably that;

they're worn. Today she wears a vaguely hippie-like dress—burgundy gauze with some kind of Indian-style print in pink, basically formless except for the tie beneath her bosom. She flips her white flat against her heel as she looks through a stack of pages to proof.

"You've got a lot of pages there," I say. If I can't work I might as well distract her.

Lynette's workload can be interpreted in a number of ways. One, she's falling behind and will be fired. Two, they are loading on the work, hoping she'll quit under the burden of an unmanageable load. If this doesn't work, they'll start to withhold projects, hoping to bore her into quitting. Eventually, if they really want to, they can find some reason to fire her.

She doesn't look up. "Stan asked me to look at it—it's not my project. I guess he wants another opinion."

My desk is suspiciously clean. Nothing in the inbox and only the map spread out like a cool blotter. Why didn't Stan ask my opinion? I'm starting to worry when Elaine comes in with three fat folders.

"Were you feeling neglected, baby?" she says.

I smile and nod. "Bring it on," I say.

She dumps the folders in my box. "It's the Titleman handbook. More changes."

"When?" I say.

"Tomorrow." She raises her eyebrows at me and leaves.

"Job security is a wonderful thing," I say, suddenly motivated. Because I'm senseless with gratitude for the work, after that moment of paranoia, I invite Lynette to lunch.

"I brought mine." She nods at the crumpled paper bag in her inbox. Judging by the wrinkles, I suspect she reuses the bag. I imagine she might reuse the plastic sandwich bags, too, rinsing them in the sink, letting them dry overnight in the dish rack so they can hold more carrot sticks, more peanut-butter-and-jelly sandwiches.

"Maybe another time," I say. My face feels hot. I pretend to look at the map, but really I'm staring at the lap of my new suit. The suit is slate blue, and I spent too much on it. Elaine and I went shopping last Thursday after work. The suit cost over three hundred, and I felt powerful buying it. It looked good; it fit just right. Now, in front of Lynette in her falling-apart white flats, it embarrasses me. I wonder when she last bought herself something new.

Lynette has pictures of her kids taped on the wall over her desk. Blond, big teeth; eyeglasses on the boy. I bet she spends most of her money on them. Maybe she's saving, too, for college. "How old are your kids, Lynette?"

She smiles in a way that is different than I've ever seen her smile. She looks at their pictures; her voice is soft. "Sealie is twelve, and Bender is ten. They go to the Friends School."

I can't tell from their names which is the girl and which is the boy. I vaguely remember hearing about the Friends School, reading an article in the paper about new techniques. There was a photograph of children kneading bread. Or maybe that was another school.

"Is that sort of New Age . . . or is it a charter school?" I ask.

Lynette's face shuts down; the softness disappears. "It's Quaker," she says. She turns her chair away from me and goes back to work.

I dial Julius's extension. The digital clock on the phone starts blinking seconds as soon as I pick up the receiver. It's a new feature, to help us keep track of time spent on personal calls. Julius and I were the first in our group to have the new phones. Now we mostly walk down the hallway to talk to each other, or meet in the stairwell.

His voicemail picks up. I suddenly wish I needed him for something more urgent than lunch. "Jules," I say, trying to fool myself at least, "call me when you get this."

Jules and I sit at our favorite restaurant. We order cosmopolitans and Greek salads.

"Yummy," I say, after my first sip. I start to feel awake for the first time today.

"How's your flower child working out?"

I roll my eyes. "Such a grind. In at seven, stays 'til seven. She brings her lunch."

He nods. "So you dislike her because she works hard and packs her lunch." Julius laughs—a short, loud *ha* that startles the overplucked women at the table next to us. Out of the corner of my eye I see them flinch.

I lean in closer, speaking softly, hoping to encourage him to do the same. "She depresses me." I wrinkle my nose. "The way she dresses . . ."

Julius gives me an incredulous look, and I know I've said something bad. "If you were my child, I'd spank you," he says. "We can't all be skinny white girls in Tahari suits, now can we?"

"Is it my fault?" I say. "Did I tell her to have those buck-toothed babies?"

He raises his eyebrows. "I call for a subject change, because you is mean, girl."

I dip my finger in and out of the condensation on my water glass. "Maybe I should take the suit back."

Jules shrugs. "If it'll make you feel better." He looks away, at the other people in the restaurant, at the TV behind the bar.

"You think I should?" I need Jules to make me feel better, not to tell me what's right.

"If you can afford it, you should enjoy it. If you can't enjoy it, then take the dang thing back and donate the money to your favorite charity." He shakes his head at me. "I've never met anyone who worries the way you do."

We finish our drinks, but we haven't touched our salads. I look with regret at the feta cheese on top of mine. I'll be hungry later. Jules gets his to go. "You should eat that," he says.

I shake my head. I'm not sure if I'm not eating to spite Jules or myself. We don't talk on the walk back. I give Jules an anemic wave at the elevators, and I take the stairs. At the landing, I sit for a moment and try to adjust my attitude. I realize there's not enough time, so I go back to my office. When I return, Lynette is there, talking on the phone with quiet intensity. "I can't talk here," she says. "I'll call tonight." She hangs up and sighs. "Ex-husbands suck. Don't get yourself one."

"Okay," I say. "I'll try not to."

*   *   *

By three thirty, we're dug in. I've taken off my jacket and shoes and sit editing in my skirt and silk shell. Lynette has put her hair up using two number-two pencils as chopsticks. We work and work. At six thirty, I'm halfway through the stack Elaine gave me. The map is long gone but will probably reappear next week after it's gone through more changes. I don't think I can sit still anymore and I'm about to slam down my pencil when Stan comes in. He's been nearby an awful lot lately. I squint at him.

"Ladies," Stan says.

"Stan the man," Lynette says.

I stare hard at Lynette's back. Stan sits in the chair next to her desk. He nods at the mess of papers.

"How's that?"

Lynette leans back, stretches her arms over her head. "I feel so fulfilled," she says.

Stan grins at her, and he's looking—really looking—at Lynette's face, her neck, her breasts. Maybe she can't see it because of the way his eyelids scrunch up whenever he's laughing or grinning, delighted or horny. I know the look. It flashes into my head that I've walked in on them in the break room a couple of times, Stan murmuring something to her and laughing. I ignored it. He invites her out with us. She accepts.

She calls her mother to say she's working late, can she watch the kids? It doesn't take long to organize. We gather in the hall, where a holiday atmosphere prevails. Stan looks pleased Lynette deems his company worthwhile. His cheeks are glowing, and he smiles faintly in Lynette's direction, listening to every word she says, as if he expects brilliant wit and wisdom to issue from her mouth. I schlump along behind the group, which is laughing too loud. Jules especially. He walks slightly behind Lynette and keeps his hand lightly at her lower back. I've just spent the entire day with this woman and I don't think she's that interesting. The inside of me feels like one big sneer.

We take Lynette straight to Earl's, bypassing the fern bar where we usually begin. Earl takes to her right away.

"Earl," she says, after they shake hands. "Do you mind if I take off my shoes and pantyhose?"

Earl's black face shines with sweat and he beams at her. "Take it all off if you want to." They both laugh.

"Make those drinks right," she says, "and I just might."

This is a side of Lynette I haven't seen. In fact, everything feels unfamiliar tonight. Instead of playing pool, we sit in a line at the bar. I'm in the dead zone, at the end, next to Jules, who turns slightly inward, toward the middle, blocking my access. Lynette orders Bud in a can, something one should not be able to get in a bar. Stan pauses, then orders the same. And so it goes. Elaine changes from white wine spritzer to Bud. Julius says, "What the hell, I'll have the same." Earl stops at me, points his finger. "What about you, baby doll?"

"Sloe gin fizz," I say.

Earl chuckles "All right, baby doll."

It's the Bud or Lynette's presence that changes the conversation. From what I can hear at my end, it sounds like they're talking about Vietnam. Stan went, infantry. I didn't know that. Julius had an uncle who went, got addicted to drugs, came home, got clean, and started a halfway house for vets. I didn't know that either. Lynette, it turns out, edited a book of stories by Vietnam vets about their experiences. I have nothing to say about any of this.

I excuse myself to the bathroom—not that anyone hears me—and let myself out the back door. I walk past downtown, which is quiet and dark on this weeknight, to my bar—The Town Hall. I don't go for company, though I do sometimes meet men there—the kind who are impressed by my youth and the excess of my bosom. I understand this. I like being wanted, being useful.

Behind the bar Christmas lights illuminate plastic poinsettias—all year round. I sit at the place where last February a college freshman carved his name. He had enormous brown eyes, and his face looked new and blank. Nothing about his expression changed, not when I put my hand on his thigh and squeezed, not later in my car when I took off my blouse, then my bra. He reminded me of sweet bland pudding, the kind you have when you're home sick from school, and you need something nourishing, flavorless, and mild.

The bartender here doesn't call me baby doll, and he doesn't know my name. He looks as old as Stan, though no wool trousers and pressed shirts for him; he wears blue jeans and t-shirts, usually red. As he pours my vodka and cranberry, I ask, "Were you in Vietnam?" He doesn't answer or look at me. It's as if I haven't spoken. He leaves my drink in front of me, yanks a bag of chips off the display rack, and settles himself against the bar. Months ago I stopped trying to charm him. He never returned my smiles. I think he recognizes me for what I am—whatever that is. He's never acknowledged what he must be aware of—the men I leave with—so I stopped caring what he thinks. He's the guy who brings my drinks.

A couple sits in the far corner at a booth. The man is older, maybe in his forties. His fingers, wrapped around his mug of beer, are thick. I like the way he looks—a little rough but quiet. I can only see the back of his woman. She's skinny, with orange-blond hair. Strawberry blonde, a nicer person would call her.

Tonight, nothing seems more important than getting the thick-fingered man away from his date or wife or whoever she is. I wonder what he does in bed, how he makes use of those fingers. I imagine we'll never make it to bed. Our contact will take place against the wall in the room next to the restrooms, with the mop in its bucket leaning beside me, the cherry smell of disinfectant in our noses. I take my drink and move to a table near them, behind the woman. I stare at him frankly—you can't be subtle in these things, I've noticed—but I can't tell if he sees me. His gaze seems to glance off me and flicker away. I take off my suit jacket and drape it over my chair. I cross my legs and lean forward. The man gets up and walks toward the bathrooms. I follow.

I try the door, but it's locked. I can hear him peeing. "Hang on a minute," he says.

I wait.

He opens the door, looks confused. "This is the men's room. Ladies' is next door."

I don't move from the doorway. "I know where it is," I say. "I know where I am." I put my hand on his belly, right above his belt buckle, and give him a gentle push into the restroom. He lets me, and I close the door behind us. I lift my skirt to my waist, slide my panties down to my ankles and off. These I stuff in the front pocket of his jeans. My hand lingers there.

"Oh my," he says softly. He puts his hands on my naked hips, gently. "That's real flattering," he says. "You're a pretty girl." He's looking down at my face and he's patting and squeezing my hip in a way that doesn't usually precede sexual contact, but suggests instead the comforting gestures one would make to a frightened animal.

"Pretty girls don't need old men like me." He pulls my skirt down and pats my hip some more. My eyes start to fill. "Don't cry, now. Here." He gives me my underwear. "Do you want me to call you a cab?" I shake my head. I wonder if he'll tell the woman about me. He seems decent and I guess he probably won't.

When I come out of the bathroom, the thick-fingered man and his woman are gone. It's just me and the bartender. I'll have one drink—I deserve that at least—before I head home. Before I get to the bar, the bartender has another waiting for me. He waits, too, hands on his hips.

"So, did you score?"

I can't tell if he's laughing at me. I don't think he is—he sounds strangely gentle—but I decide not to answer.

"I didn't think so. Duane's pretty straitlaced." He sits on a stool behind the bar and looks at the TV. "Kids today," he says and shakes his head.

I don't think he means to insult me, but I feel I should pretend to be outraged. It's probably this unusual failure of mine that's made him so chatty. "You're just full of conversation, aren't you?"

He shrugs. "Just curious." His arms are folded. He's slim. I start to wonder about possibilities, but stop myself. I can't handle more rejection tonight, especially from the bartender. I dig in my purse for money. I'm thinking of ways to make it up to myself—maybe a bubble bath and some Chambord until I'm foggy. I put down my cash and he covers my hand with his. "Where you going so fast?" he says. My heart beats a little faster, and I tremble at what I want to happen. He lets go of my hand, and he comes around to the customer side of the bar. Standing close, he speaks so softly I'm not sure later if he spoke at all. "I'll take care of you. Is that what you want?"

I nod.

"Sit down," he says. "Drink your drink." He locks the front door with the keys hanging off his belt loop. "Hey, turn off the TV." He points to the remote on the bar and walks to the jukebox. Leadbelly starts up with "Irene." He wipes a rag over the tables and puts up the chairs. I expect the regulars will be disappointed to find their bar closed early, but I can't care about them. Instead, I finish my drink. When he's finished washing his hands, he comes to me and kisses me deeply.

"Mmmm," I say, reaching for his belt.

"In the back," he says.

We go in the back, to a small room with a bed. I find this sad but not so sad that I can't keep up. We fall asleep around five in the morning.

When I wake up, I know I'm missing work. I roll out of bed and walk naked to the bar. The floor feels grimy on my bare feet so I walk back, on tippy-toes, and put on my pumps. I shiver in the cool air. At the bar, in the dim morning light, I fix myself a vodka-cranberry. I'm all gooseflesh, and a little wobbly, too. I bump against the doorjamb on my way back, and my drink sloshes over my hand. I lick it off—sweet, sharp, salt. When I return, he's awake, his forearm thrown across his eyes. I kick off my pumps and climb on top of him.

"Drinking so early," he says. "Hard-core. Did you have a nice time last night?"

"Did it sound like I had a nice time?"

"I think those were good sounds."

"I'll come back tonight, if you're around."

"I should be," he says.

I look around the small room at his personal things—the jar of change on the dresser, the bottle of water on the floor next to the bed, the unplugged digital clock on the windowsill. I set my drink on the floor next to his water and get under the sheet with him. He doesn't say, "I have things to do, errands to run, a sick mother, a jealous girl-friend." Instead, he turns to me drowsily, pulls us together. For a second I imagine Lynette's desk, the crumpled paper bag in the corner, the fat file folders piled next to her chair on the floor. I see Elaine at her desk, hear her sigh when she realizes I'm not coming in today. Then I see my desk: empty, clean. I part my lips to meet his and my body feels light and warm, like a patch of sunlight on his.

Every Year the Baby Dies

Every year the baby dies. This one at least made it home from the hospital. They sit at the kitchen table, mother and baby, while outside the sun sears through the dew. Inside, the room is dim and slightly cool from the night. A cup of cold coffee sits on the table in its white saucer. Next to the coffee sits the baby's bottle, the formula froth having given way hours ago to a ring of bubbles. The baby won't eat. Gini sighs and sips her coffee. The baby's eyes are closed, and she thinks this one looks like a baby bird: beakish face, the way the cheeks and mouth fall away from the nose. She can't see anything wrong with it.

Frank will be in soon for breakfast, which he will get himself, unless she puts the baby in its crib. She hears him now in the bathroom, rinsing his razor, tapping it on the porcelain. Her elder daughter won't be up for another hour or so. She wonders if the daughter in her arms will ever wear dresses. It's funny, she thinks, how long it takes to make one—a baby, not a dress. The dresses are easy. For babies, nine months of nausea, bloating, fatigue. Then they slip away so quickly, in a mere fraction of an unguarded moment. One minute she's in the kitchen reaching into the spice cabinet for parsley, a vibrant, healthy mother, wife of a virile young man with teeth so white he looks like a movie star, and the next she's standing over the crib of a blue infant. One minute she's in the backyard, holding a plate for the meat her husband grills, laughing at her neighbor's joke, and the next she's holding the telephone in the kitchen, twisting the cord, calling the ambulance.

The girl seems unaffected. She doesn't understand; she's only five, after all. The nuns tell her something—what is it? The babies are baptized right away, in the hospital, so they don't have to talk about the cold comfort of limbo. That's it—the babies go straight to heaven to play with Baby Jesus.

The phone rings. She glances at it and shifts the baby. It's her mother, she knows, calling to offer assistance, or her mother-in-law with offers of the same. She avoids looking at the casserole dishes on the counter—the lasagna and eggplant they delivered, which she was too tired to put away, which she is supposed to eat to keep her strength up, as if keeping her strength up will somehow make the baby live. It's not her strength at issue—never has been. It's the babies that die. She never even feels sick. The phone keeps ringing. If she doesn't answer, her father—or her father-in-law—will arrive within minutes to investigate.

"'lo," she says.

It's her mother-in-law.

"I'm fine. We're fine."

The baby's eyes are still closed. The lids appear ruddy and soft. All her babies have been small, and this one is too. It hasn't uncurled itself, which she thinks could be a bad sign. Shouldn't it be stretching its limbs? Last year's baby—the boy—had come out wailing and waving its skinny arms. It screamed and kicked and struck out throughout its first three months. They had been hopeful. They had named that baby. The new baby sighs and hugs its arms tighter to its chest. We'll just see, she'd said to Frank in the hospital. We'll see what we think when we get home. She tried to sound cheerful. We'll let her grow into her name.

The mother-in-law wonders how the new bottles are working. The bottles are fine, the nipples are fine; it's the baby that won't cooperate. Gini only thinks this last, but somehow the mother-in-law hears it. Make the milk warmer, she suggests, or cooler. Has she tried the new formula? She has. Eat, the mother-in-law says. Keep your strength up.

Yes, she says. Babies can sense when the mother is nervous. Keep eating, keep sleeping: make everything as normal as possible. Do not become hysterical.

She imagines a switch flipping. Hysteria would feel like a vacation. She imagines herself in bed, soothed by the balm of insensibility. No one could expect anything of her then. Why don't you come for coffee later, she says. I'll bring cake, the mother-in-law says. Lovely, Gini says, and they hang up.

She walks the baby to the back door, peers outside at the patio and the grill and the small trees that are growing up with the neighborhood. The girl's tricycle sits in the grass, its front wheel canted toward the door. The little streamers hanging from the handlebars whip in the breeze. She should get laundry in but she can go another day and no one will think ill of her. This is your backyard, she says to the baby. We're thinking about a pool someday. She holds the baby more snugly. The doctor has told her to put the baby down more, that holding it too much could cause problems later. Their eyes locked on *later*, as if agreeing on a future could ensure one. You have a nice older sister, she tells the baby. She's waited so long for a playmate.

She feels herself getting weepy, which is not what she wants. She can't have her husband see her cry; it will only make him worry, and he has enough to worry about. Listen, she says to the baby. Tell me what you want. She touches a finger to its cheek. It reminds her of an egg yolk, soft and barely contained. I'll do anything. Just tell me.

If this baby dies, there won't be another. After the last boy died, she decided that Frank couldn't take it anymore. Already, he is less invested in this one. He hasn't held her, and when Gini's holding her he keeps his distance. This one is God's will, but after this, it will be Gini's will. She hasn't discussed this with Frank, and she won't, but she knows he feels the same way. She'll make sure it doesn't happen again, and she won't involve him in the details. People can assume whatever they like: that she can't have any more children; that they have chosen to stop trying. Who would blame them?

Listen, she says to the baby. I need to know. Are you sticking around? The baby opens its eyes: slate blue water. She appears to search out the origin of the voice. Her little shrimp lips work against each other, and for the first time, she wiggles in her mother's arms. Then she makes a face. She squeezes her eyes shut, pulls her lips into a grimace, and wrinkles her tiny nose.

OK, Gini says. We'll see. You should know, we're good people. You'd like us. We have good parties. This is a nice neighborhood. See what you think.

The baby arches her back and cries without making a sound. Gini knows that none of this can be taken as a sign.

⚜

"The Catholics had their baby," she says, across the rim of her teacup. "Another one."

John doesn't know why she insists on referring to them as "the Catholics"; she knows their names, has been to their house for cookouts, even attended the christening of the elder girl. He doesn't put the newspaper down. "Yes," he says. "Frank told me. He called while you were getting your hair done."

"I guess I should bring something over," she says. "That's what they do."

"That's what a lot of people do," he says. He cut himself just over the lip this morning, shaving with a shaky hand. He was over Frank and Gini's last night for a quick, celebratory drink—in the basement bar, so as not to disturb mother and baby. As Frank led the way, John peered down the hall, hoping to catch a glimpse of Gini. Already he felt a difference in the household, a tenuous dreamlike quality: the trance that falls on a house when a baby arrives.

"Anyway, I'm sure they're fine. They have a lot of family in town. You needn't bring anything."

She sighs her impatience at him. "It's what's done. I have to."

He longs to tell her she plays the martyr, that the role doesn't suit her. He thinks the meaning would be lost on her—not that she's dumb. She'd be insulted by the religious aspect of it.

"What's so funny?" she wants to know.

"You," he says. He sips the orange juice she has put out for him. He'll eat the breakfast she prepared while she smokes across the table.

She's probably already thinking about errands she has to run—the market, the dry cleaner, the Ladies' Guild—and she's impatient for him to get to work. He almost wishes she wouldn't bother with the breakfasts. The butter Tuesday was rancid, and today he thinks he sees a faint sprinkle of mold across his rye toast. The children don't fare any better: sugar cereal and a glass of milk. On weekends he prepares eggs and waffles, but during the week, the three of them are at her mercy. Last night's dinner: brown bread from a can with tuna fish hash, something he had never heard of and never wants to see again. He often finds the children at Frank and Gini's kitchen table, stuffing themselves with homemade cookies or bread. They always come away with something for him—a plate of lasagna, a bottle of homemade wine or the fennel-sweet sausages Gini's mother makes. He has warned the children to stay away from the house, because of the new baby, whom they are eager to see.

He glances across at his wife while she scratches at the slender notepad on which she writes her lists. She has little need for nourishment—any old morsel will do. She drinks coffee and eats one piece of toast for breakfast. For lunch, it's canned peaches and cottage cheese. As the seasons change and different fruits and vegetables arrive at the market, her diet remains unchanged. Once, he went to the market with her when he was on vacation over the summer. He bought a bag of yellow peaches and ate one every day at lunch while she sat across from him eating her canned fruit. When he offered her a slice from the blade of his knife, she literally turned up her nose. "Darling," she said, "your hillbilly ways tell during the summer. Next you'll want the children to go without shoes." At the time, he'd thought this funny. He'd laughed, and so had she. He'd grown up picking apples, peaches, huckleberries—whatever grew outside and could be eaten—with his brothers and sisters in West Virginia. He had climbed a tree for her once, to pick apple blossoms for her hair before some Yale dance or other, or after the dance when they were just drunk enough. She agreed to marry him shortly after. He'd imagined fruit trees in their backyard in Connecticut, and four or five children running barefoot through the clover. She agreed to one crabapple and two children. He feels a pang for his mother's cornbread and preserves, and a big glass of buttermilk. A stone the size of a peach pit rises and lodges in his throat.

"What are you writing?" he asks.

"I have to give a speech at the Ladies' Guild lunch today," she says.

"What's it about?"

Her weary look tells him he is interfering. "It's about fund-raising. For the library."

"I see. A worthy cause."

He brings the uneaten toast and his juice glass to the sink.

"Don't bother," she says. "I'll get it." She doesn't look up from her notepad.

He wonders what she does all day. Often when he comes home he finds her on the telephone. The conversations end abruptly, the way the nurses in his ward halt their talk when he comes by. Her tone is often incredulous or conspiratorial; he assumes gossip. He thinks about the nurses at the ward, their crisp ways. She, too, has her ways.

He kisses her dryly on the temple as she writes. It's Friday, and he wants—needs—something different, something more. He holds her shoulder—so small and hard. "Let's have a picnic at the beach tonight."

She puts her pen down. "What's wrong with you?"

He knows her concern is genuine; she views deviation from routine as a harbinger of illness or swift moral decline. He's surprised to find himself gripping her shoulder tighter, to keep his hand from shaking. The shaking travels up his arm.

"Summer's almost over. Can't you give your hillbilly husband leave this once?"

Her lips part. She's not dumb. "What would you like in your basket?"

"Cornbread." He knows she'll buy a box of Jiffy mix, but it will be something, some vestige of what he's known.

"Oh, John—really? It's a hundred degrees and you want me to use the oven?"

"Please."

She shakes her head. "All right."

Outside he hails Frank, who has started his truck and is heading for work. Frank flashes him that smile—that dazzling smile. They shake hands through the pickup's window.

"So far, so good," Frank says, then winces.

"The children are very excited about their new playmate. How's Gini?"

"Good," he nods. "She's good."

He would like to invite them along on the picnic, but he knows that's impossible. The baby is too new and everything now so precarious. Just for a moment, the invisible mask that holds Frank together breaks. "Every time it happens," he says, "it's always her. She always finds them."

John says the worst thing, commits the biggest sin. "It won't happen this time. God's not that cruel." He's surprised by the force of his anger. His heart pounds, and he's sure his face is flushed. He's never seen Frank tired; the area around his eyes looks soft and pale compared to the rest of his face, which is deeply tanned from working outdoors. The white creases in the corners of his eyes look like the sign of perpetual wincing. Frank nods and puts the truck in gear. John pats the hood, and the two men part.

As he walks across the lawn to his car, he has a moment of animal joy, and it shames him. He feels it in the time it takes to complete one step: he rises up, for he bounces slightly when he walks, and feels wild gratitude for his good fortune, which has nothing to do with his virtue or God's plan. He's simply biologically fortunate to have children who live. He relishes this. The sun shines, the grass is lush and green, his children are healthy. His other leg swings forward, and he feels sick in his gut. The whole landscape has gone yellow. He's lucky—that's all.

To chase away these feelings, he thinks about the day ahead, specifically the patient who thinks she's Mary Magdalene. Every morning she prepares a basin of water. She folds a towel over her arm and waits in a chair by the door of her room. She won't eat. At lunchtime, she empties the basin and refills it. She won't last much longer without food. He has talked to her about this. What gives your body strength?

He does, the woman said. Food gives your body strength, he said. You need nourishment to perform your duties. He gestured to the basin. She placed her dry hand on his and patted it. He thought this a sign that she would eat and felt elated to have reached her. Later when he saw her untouched plate, he swore aloud. Today he wonders if she will be able to get out of bed. He suspects the nurses will perform her ritual for her. Years ago he would have found this an indulgence of ignorant superstition; but when faced with chance, why *not* ritual and superstition? Care, vigilance, and rectitude take one only so far. Do everything right, and it's still not enough.

Inside his sedan, it's hot. In a different life, in West Virginia, he would be fishing now. His children would run barefoot outside, getting stung by insects, eating berries off the vine, swimming in sumptuous spring-fed creeks. He thinks he will stop at the nursery on the way home for a fruit tree—maybe peach or apple, maybe apricot. Apricots ripen suddenly, he remembers, and it's a race to get them before the birds do, to can them before they spoil. He remembers the bathtub at home full of them, mounds and mounds of miniature setting suns, and his mother and sisters in the kitchen, their long hair pulled back, banks of steam rising from the big pots. Gini would know how to put up. Maybe he would demand it of his wife, that much anyway.

❦

The girl grips the wooden rails of the crib in her small hands. She stares hard at the new baby, watching its midsection rise and fall. Sometimes the baby touches one slender finger to its undershirt. Its lips are open slightly. The baby sighs harshly and stretches out against the mattress. Angels come for the babies, Sister Catherine told her. They go straight to God. She doesn't know why God needs them. They are pretty. Maybe He likes to have pretty things. They are pretty, but she needs a brother or sister, the way her friends have. When they finish playing, the neighbor children go together into their house. She goes to hers alone. She had a dream about Baby Francis, that she woke up, raced to his room and found him asleep in his bed. They floated up to the ceiling together holding hands. She had never felt so light. She has heard the neighbor children fight—over toys or who got the bigger piece of cake. She would never fight with Francis. She would give him anything he wanted. She would make him pancake breakfasts to coax him from bed. She would take him to the playground, let him use her toys and books. When she woke from her dream she threw back the covers and ran down the hall. As soon as she saw the pale blue walls of his room and the curtains that hadn't been shut, she remembered. Baby Francis went to heaven. All the babies went straight to heaven to be with Jesus. He loves them and looks after them. They sing with the other angels and they float on clouds. They are happy.

The baby keeps breathing. She's been watching since naptime started over an hour ago. She thinks if she keeps watching, this one will be all right. The thing is she's been up for an hour and hasn't been to the bathroom. She really has to go. And she's hungry—no breakfast yet. Pop went to work. Mother had been in the kitchen, rattling the lids of casserole dishes and opening the refrigerator. She went to the basement to put a load of laundry in and then went silent. The girl thinks she must have gone back to bed. She does sometimes. This time when they came home from the hospital they looked tired. She leapt from the couch, where she'd been playing cards with Nonny, and ran to greet them. She thought they looked sorry about something, but she had known not to ask, just to smile and be happy to see them and the new baby.

This baby is small, but no smaller than the others. "Get big," she whispers. She thinks she can slip away to the bathroom. It won't take long. She wants to ask God to watch the baby while she's gone, but she's afraid. God might see the baby and like it and take it away to be with Him. So she doesn't ask. She means to be quick. She hears the neighbor children playing outside, so she stands on the toilet to watch them out the window. They splash water at each other in a large metal tub. The girl has a pink swimsuit. The boy wears cut-off dungarees. They will take her berry-picking later. She uses the fancy soap her mother keeps for guests. The soap makes lots of bubbles. She thinks she will check on the baby and get dressed. Then she'll check on the baby again and take the egg timer outside. That way she'll know to come in before too long.

She can't stop herself: she thinks about the first baby as she's looking at the new baby. She scrunches up her face to make it disappear, but she has the sound her mother made inside her—a scream that can't come out, the sound she makes when she's having a nightmare. The baby didn't look right. She thought it had eaten the blue roses off a cake from Libby's because its lips were blue, and she was angry because no one had told her about any cake. Mother swept a finger inside the baby's mouth, the way Pop takes the hook out of a fish. Then mother made the sound. Pop came running. He turned the baby upside down by its ankles and swatted its back. He had done this once to her, when a piece of hard candy slid down her throat. She was upside down, the candy shooting across the kitchen and clattering into the sink, before she knew she was choking. Nothing came out of the baby. The ambulance came.

She sits in the small rocker and watches. She can't stop herself: she makes the face Pop calls "cross." She wants the baby to stay with her, but what if Jesus wants the baby? Isn't that nice for the baby? Jesus has wanted so many of their babies to play with in heaven. Why hasn't He wanted her? Has she been bad? She tries to be good. She will have to try harder.

She squeezes the wooden bars of the crib until her hands burn. The baby breathes. It flaps its tiny fingers at the air. She doesn't know yet if it's an angel or a friend.

Chestnut Season

Traffic on this stretch of road slows to a crawl at 8:00 AM. Exhaust from the car in front of you billows out in frosty puffs while you sip your coffee. As you sip you look across your knuckles at the gleaming garnet ring on your third finger. For now, the ring is a sign that everything is A-OK. A curly strand of your hair has caught in the setting. Gross, you think, as you pick it out. You shake your hair, catch it up in your hand, and gently pull out a few dozen strands. Very gross, you think, but you hum along to whatever oldie is on the radio. You have surrounded yourself with many signs that things are A-OK and getting better: your super-clean Volkswagen Beetle; the gold locket with your grandmother's photo; the red sweater set from Ann Taylor; the right highlights for your chestnut hair; the smart, upbeat guy you became engaged to Christmas Eve, who gave you the garnet ring.

Stopped at the light two miles from your office, you glance at the car next to yours and see yourself—ten years from now. You've put on weight, but it's you—you recognize the profile. What has happened, you wonder, and you feel a rock of fear in your chest. Your future self looks haggard: the hair's the same, minus correct highlights, but you have multiple chins. You wear what appears to be a flannel nightshirt. Much has happened to bring you to this state—a person who drives around in her pajamas, in an old white Ford with rust, no less.

Maybe what your mother said is true: that you're uppity and you'll get yours someday. Quite clearly you remember all the unlovely things she's said to you and that you've said to her: they surge up inside you like an army of red-hot pins. In high school she mocked you: "You clump around in those high heels, girly, like you know what you're doing. You ain't got a clue." Her boyfriend, the handsome one who smelled nice when he kissed you goodnight that one time, was over on the couch with her, both of them with martinis. "Damn you," you said, without the conviction or authority for damning. "You bitch," you said—a statement of fact. Now you think, how can a girl who damns her mother—her own mother—ever come to any good?

The light changes. You creep along next to your future self, glancing over from time to time. You catch your future self drinking a giant Slurpee through a maraschino-red straw. You groan—no wonder you're fat. You try to determine if your future self could be happy with this arrangement, and you attempt to concoct a scenario where that might be possible. Maybe this is your vacation and you are indulging yourself just this little bit, with the Super Big Gulp Slurpee and the early-morning ride in pajamas. You squint. Happiness seems unlikely here.

On the other hand, maybe you've had a run of bad luck: You've been laid off, through no fault of your own. Your husband has become ill, and you can no longer rely on his income. You have become ill, and you battle back from your illness. Your friends say, "So brave." They murmur about your toughness and strength. Tears well on your lower eyelids. You turn your weepy gaze on your future self to find her talking on her cell phone. She holds a list in one hand, the phone with the other, and steers with her ample knees. You wipe your tears away. The woman on the phone talks, lays her list across the steering wheel, and crosses one item off while holding the pen cap in her mouth. She re-caps the pen, inserting it into the cap in her mouth, all the while continuing to talk on the phone and steer with her knees. No, you think, this woman is not rebounding from a long illness—that much is clear.

You suspect you have done something terrible to bring about this change in fortune. Maybe you're not as smart as you think you are, and you have done something irrevocably stupid. Where is the super-clean Volkswagen Beetle? Where is the Ann Taylor sweater set? Where is the garnet ring? What if, as the result of your previously unknowable stupidity, you have ruined your life and lost everything good?

This has not occurred to you before. What if there are things you want but can't have? What if you can only go so far? You thought you'd go as far as you wanted at work. Have you misjudged your status there? You imagine that your boss has been compiling a list of your faults; one day he will call you in to a meeting at which he will expose you for what you are—a mediocre intellect, a frivolous girl who happens to be rather mean and shallow, suspicious and anal-retentive, controlling.

You examine your fiancé under the lens of this new microscope. What is that look he gives you, the one that annoys you so? It's the I'm-not-really-here look; the body is taking up space, but behind his face, you imagine your fiancé's brain works on scenarios that have nothing to do with you: his career path, for instance—where he'll be in five years, ten; what he will say to his boss when they play golf together on Saturday; when he will go back to school, where, and for which degree; burgundy dress shoes—something other than black or brown, something that will set him apart from the others; a woman who works down the hall, a blonde who sings karaoke and has big white teeth; a convertible, someday, and this blonde's curly hair streaming out from under a scarf as she beams at him from the passenger seat. Yes, you're sure now that your fiancé is someone who thinks of burgundy dress shoes and golf, and blondes with big teeth, while you are talking about wedding and honeymoon plans, houses and crystal, DJs and swing bands.

The armpits of your Ann Taylor sweater set feel damp, clammy. The valley between your breasts has grown hot, and now a tropical climate emerges there, beneath your sweater—humid and suffocating. That woman next to you leans forward to turn up the radio, having relinquished the phone. She taps her thumbs on the steering wheel, sings along, accidentally hits the horn, flinches, laughs. You wonder what station she is listening to. At the next light, you put your car in park and jerk up the brake. You get out of your bug and stretch, looking at the Ford as you might survey a wreck that's holding up traffic. Your future self doesn't notice your approach; in fact, she doesn't see you at all until you rap your knuckle on the window. She jumps, rolls down the window.

"Yes?" she says.

You see that this woman is wholly different from yourself. In the backseat lie plastic grocery bags. One bag has spilled open, and a riot of party gear splashes across the seat: cone-shaped motley hats; tissue paper crackers in pink and orange; tiny flesh-colored ballerina candleholders; cans of spray frosting; a paper pin-the-tail-on-the-donkey, one sheepish-looking heavily-lashed donkey eye peering at you from beneath its plastic wrapper. The woman who is not you will bake a cake later, for her daughter. She will write her little girl's name in icing across the cake. Maybe she will spray the leftover frosting into her mouth before she cleans up the kitchen, showers, gets ready for the party. That night, seven little candles will glow over the cake, held aloft by the tiny plastic ballerinas. After the candles have been blown out, mother and daughter will lick frosting from the silver feet of the ballerinas. Relief washes over you, sort of, but it prickles.

The inside of the Ford smells like the woman's cherry Slurpee and underneath that, once-damp floormats. The woman waits for you, but you say nothing. You want to ask, "Can I come to the party?" What you finally say is, "I'm sorry."

This woman, whom you're beginning to like, smiles and says, "It's cold."

You straighten and look down the road at the line of cars behind the Ford. A man in a suit and tie and overcoat dials someone on his cell phone from the seat of his Bronco. You walk back to your car having just not met your future self. You mull over the not-nice things you've imagined and recalled about yourself. Does a Frivolity Scale exist, and where would you fall on it if one did? How smart are you, really? And what about your fiancé? If you're shallow, mean, and anal-retentive, why is he marrying you? Your own mother doesn't like you, and you've never wondered why. These things you haven't ever thought about follow behind you as you drive to work, like a piece of ribbon hanging from a cat's rear end. It trails you for the rest of day, hard to shake.

What Nina Wants

Mingus hates my whistling, and he's not crazy about my singing either. Mingus— who is my husband, not jazz legend Charles Mingus—shakes his head at me. I can't help myself, though, as we drive along the Pacific Coast Highway with the top down. I project my voice out over the rocks, in the direction of the barking seals—dark, shiny, and wet— sunning themselves on the rocks below. He can't possibly hear. I can hardly hear myself because of the wind, because of Ella Fitzgerald and Louis Armstrong crooning from the speakers, because my red silk scarf covers my hair and, ridiculously, my ears. He can no doubt tell from my gestures and my posture that I am singing. His pale lips are pressed together, and his sunglasses hide his eyes. He looks blank. Squaring my shoulders, I sit up straighter in the tiny passenger seat of our rented MG. I toss my head and gesture to the seals. My splayed fingers slice the air into ribbons that trail behind us. I sing louder.

"You look ridiculous," he says, finally.

Underneath the scarf my hair is in curlers. I wear a yellow halter dress and sunglasses that cover half my face. My high-heeled sandals are bright red.

"You know it takes forever for my hair to curl."

He sighs. He knows he has to accommodate me. If I am to believe that he, Rob McAllister, a thirty-year-old trust-fund volunteer at the

Smithsonian, is actually jazz legend Charles Mingus, then he has to accept that I am Julliard-educated singer and pianist Nina Simone, who has black hair and must leave curlers in all day for the curl to take.

"Well," he says, "just don't go waving your gun around the party like you did last time."

"I hate it when people talk during the music," I say, and we smile. We're both proud of this characterization of mine, based on the true story of Nina Simone firing a gun out the window of her Paris apartment at late-night revelers who roused her from slumber. The Taurus .38 Special rests at the bottom of my purse, loaded and wrapped in a red chiffon scarf.

This is the first time in several days we've had a laugh together. We're on our way to a swank fund-raiser for the Smithsonian Jazz Orchestra somewhere near the Hearst Castle, where Rob hopes to persuade the impossibly rich to part with their money. I'm hoping to sustain this note of playfulness for the rest of our trip. In ways I hadn't expected, living the lives of our most revered legends is taking a toll, though it's supposed to save our marriage. This is what Marriage Counselor Number Three has told us: to assume the roles of people who command respect, who demand attention, who get what they want. Marriage Counselor Number Three used to be an actor. He says playing roles can be very freeing. I'm beginning to doubt him. Rob has become self-absorbed, always thinking about his music, his career. I'm determined, however, on this trip to demand his attention, to make sure we connect as much as possible as husband and wife. I turn to him, settling the skirt of my dress around my legs.

"Did you listen to the tape I left, baby?" I ask, referring to the tape of Nina Simone, recorded live in Paris, that I wrapped in a pair of lace panties and attached with a rubber band to the neck of his bass.

"Mmm, no. I've been trying to get some guys together to play. People are so unreliable. I'm tired of people who won't commit, you know what I mean?"

"Right," I say, "mm-hm."

This sounds more like Rob than Mingus. In our actual lives, Rob holes up in our basement drinking pitchers of iced tea and playing bass. He hasn't always been this way. We met in a club in Adams Morgan, where Rob played in a combo. The piano player thought he was McCoy Tyner, but it was Rob who held the group together. Over the years, Rob's friends became less reliable musical outlets. They married, had children, and moved far out into the suburbs. The arrival of McCoy Tyner's fourth baby spelled the end of Rob's music, until the edict of Marriage Counselor Number Three. I was not surprised when he chose Mingus. It took me two weeks to talk him out of taking his upright on this trip; as it is, the electric juts out of the trunk of the car. We had to affix one of my scarves to the end of it before the rental clerk would let us leave the lot.

I reach for my purse. The heft of it, with the weight of the Taurus, still surprises me. I'm just powdering my nose, but knowing it's there gives me a sense of power. A gun is a serious thing.

"What do you think about stopping for a drink somewhere?"

Rob swerves to his left and raises a cloud of dirt all around us. I wave my hand in front of my face and cough.

"Here we are," he says, stopping in front of a cedar-shingled inn. He moves to get out of the car, but I stop him with my hand on his thigh.

"Are we on the same wavelength or what?" I lean in, massaging his thigh, and give him an open-mouth kiss. He doesn't kiss back, but he doesn't pull away. He seems about to say something, and I think, this is it. This is when he gives it up, when I find out What Rob Thinks. I feel relieved, and something else I don't recognize—giddy? Delighted by the prospect of a cataclysmic fracas?

"I have to use the restroom," he says. He gets out and slams the door, walks around the back of the car, compulsively checks the rope securing his bass, then walks past my door and into the restaurant. I remain seated. I click open my purse to look at the Taurus.

We secure a room at the cedar-shingled inn so we can freshen up before the second part of our drive down the Coast Highway. Marriage Counselor Number One recommended such impromptu jaunts. She also recommended lingerie and candles. I did my best: body-skimming silk gowns and backless slippers with a froth of dyed pink feathers across the toes; lace tap pants with a split seam up the middle; garter belts and stockings in red and black; vinyl hot-pants and chain mail halters. Each time I approached Rob in my finery, he would pale and look into the distance, at some place beyond both of us. The scented candles made him short of breath. We parted ways with Marriage Counselor Number One, but not before getting a recommendation for Marriage Counselor Number Two. I was able to cram all the lingerie and scented candles into one drawer of my vanity.

In the restaurant on the first floor of the inn, I insist on sitting next to Rob in the European fashion.

"I like to stretch my legs," he says.

"You have plenty of room." I smile because the waitress has arrived. "I'll have a cosmopolitan. Two."

Rob shoots me a look. "Don't start."

I reach in my purse and he flinches. I pull out my cigarettes and he relaxes.

"I'll have a Campari and soda," he says. "You're making me nervous."

"How can you drink that shit? It tastes like bile."

"It's refreshing." He watches the door to see who comes in. Not that anyone will recognize him.

"Bullshit." I shake out my match.

"I wish you wouldn't swear." He shakes his head. "And I have to sit here while you have those curlers in your head. Jesus. Have a little self-respect."

I say nothing. I smoke. When our drinks arrive, I gulp one then the other. He looks at me. I'm a sipper, usually.

"Watch out. You're going to end up like You-Know-Who."

You-Know-Who: Marriage Counselor Number Two, who cried during our first meeting until mascara ran down her cheeks in dirty rivulets. She stank of alcohol and apologized wetly, snuffling into a shredded pink tissue for five minutes while we stood in front of our chairs trying to leave.

I get up without saying anything and head to the bar for another drink. Rob follows me, and my eyes shine at the prospect of our confrontation, but when he gets to the bar he greets an overblown woman in tan stretch pants and a tight jacket. Her hair poufs out around her head, and she has the physique of someone who should not wear stretch pants. They are talking music, something Rob does with women only when he wants to screw.

On the bartender's rubber mat sit cups of olives, bright red cherries, and short fluorescent swords. I brandish one of the little swords and stab cherries from the bartender's cup while he makes my drink. Rob settles in with the woman at the end of the bar. He has taken his characterization of Mingus too far. I should leave, but instead I keep eating cherries. Some apocryphal childhood warning about maraschino cherries comes to mind: it takes six months to digest one. What would Nina Simone do? The bartender pauses to watch me. I dangle a cherry by the stem and make to fling it at him.

"Open," I say. He does, I fling, and he catches it in his mouth. In between filling drink orders for Rob and the woman, the bartender reports back to me and I toss cherries and olives into his mouth. He has a startling rate of success.

A silver-haired man at the bar notices me. He smiles in a way that is fatherly, but not. "I like that look. Going to a party?"

I remember the curlers in my hair and nod. The silver-haired man is named Jerome, and he drinks a martini out of a glass so delicate I imagine it would be easy to take a bite from it.

"I've never had a martini," I lie.

He hands me his drink. I watch him over the rim of the glass as I sip. "Yuck."

He laughs. Jerome tells me about his daughters in college, how pretty they are, how he hopes they don't marry bums. I can see by the way Jerome rolls the cuffs of his white dress shirt under instead of over that he is not a bum. He takes care with his appearance: crisp sideburns, expensive slacks, delightful cologne. While I admire his polished skin, he asks me all about myself—what I do, where I'm from, how long Rob and I have been married, what Rob does.

"Is that him?" He gestures to the end of the bar where Rob sits talking with the woman. He's laughing at something she's said. I wonder what's so funny.

I don't look at Jerome. I sip my drink. "He's working."

Jerome changes the subject, mentions that he'd like to get his wife a present while he's away. I promise to help him pick out a scarf at the gift shop. I ask about her looks. He holds up his hands as if to illustrate.

"Almond-shaped brown eyes—big ones, set far apart; perfect little nose. Nice skin—like yours."

I didn't know I had nice skin. In the gift shop, I pick out a periwinkle square with a small floral pattern in cranberry. "It's tasteful, but vibrant. She'll like it."

I show him different ways to tie it. He shakes his head. "I'll never remember. How do you women do it?" I smile at him. Jerome appreciates even the small things, and sometimes that's all there are.

He sits with me on the porch swing. We're swinging lightly, just the tips of our shoes tapping the worn boards. Jerome and his wife have been married twenty-two years. He tells me about some jazz clubs in the area that they've been to. I barely lift an eyebrow at that. "Or maybe you and your husband would like camping or sailing." I try to smile for him. "That might be nice." I start to imagine Rob and me camping, but instead an image comes of Jerome by the campfire and his wife emerging sleepily from their tent to take the coffee he has made for her. Finally, he has to go. He gives me his phone number and address in San Jose.

"If you're in the area, I'd love for you to meet my family." He holds my hand firmly in both of his. Before letting go, he leans in close and tells me, "If you were my wife, I wouldn't be in the bar talking to another woman."

My throat feels suddenly tight, and I try to swallow the feeling. I wait on the porch swing for Rob to find me. He appears at the tail end of an exhausted dusk. He doesn't look right at me and he doesn't sit down. He just stands there, looking beyond me. I turn in the direction of his gaze. It's the dirt parking lot.

"What've you been doing?" he asks.

"Waiting for you?"

"You didn't know I was gone."

"Do we have to go to this party?" I want to watch TV until I fall asleep.

"It's my job."

"Please, you don't even get paid."

"I have responsibilities," he says.

"Thanks for telling me."

He sits on the railing across from the swing. I imagine he wishes he had married someone different. Who would he want? The stretch-pants lady? Maybe he's thinking, "I should have married *blank*."

"Listen," he says, and he looks serious. "This party tonight. No playing around."

I say nothing; I continue to rock on the swing.

"A lot of wealthy people will be there."

"What's in it for me?"

"I think we should make a pact: No drinking, no gun."

I clear my throat. "Won't people think it's weird if we're not drinking—at a party?"

"A lot of people don't drink." He looks me up and down. "Do you have something else to wear?"

I nod. "In the trunk." I get up and start for the car. I'm pretending to get our bag, but I have something else in mind. I toss my purse on the passenger seat. I untie the trunk and slide the bass out. As I walk across the highway lugging Rob's bass, I hear him shout, "Nina!" I turn and wave, all smiles. I walk off the road, onto the shoulder, stopping at the guardrail. Below, the Pacific beats against the rocks. Seals bark. I rest his bass on the guardrail. I hear him coming up behind me, his leather-soled shoes crunching the roadside gravel.

"Don't do it, Nina." His tone is not threatening, and he stops a few feet away.

I lick my lips. "Why shouldn't I?"

"Come on, Alicia." He says my name as if something larger than his bass is at stake. I can't remember when he last called me by my name. Have we really come to this?

I sit on the edge of our bed at the inn.

"Take off your shoes," Rob says.

"You're retarded," I say. "This was a bad idea."

"I know that." He goes to check on the tub he's running for me. He turns off the water and comes back, drying his hands on a small white towel. "It's ready. I'll get coffee."

I rise and squirm to unfasten my dress.

"Here," he says, "let me."

I stand still while he unzips me. He pulls the fabric from my shoulders and traces one of my moles with his forefinger. "What's going on here? You've got a continent on your shoulder."

My dress falls to my ankles and I kick it aside. "It's been there the whole damn time."

I strip in front of him, not wanting to, but not wanting to make a point of not undressing in front of him either. I leave a trail of heavy-duty foundation garments on my way to the bathroom. When I turn at the doorway, hit in the face by the steam of the bath, I see him bend to retrieve the flesh-colored brassiere and the satiny elastic girdle with the ribbon-like garters. He folds them and places them on the bed, smoothing them gently. I consider calling Marriage Counselor Number Three to tell him what a worthless quack he is, but I feel foolish for not noticing this sooner. I slide under the water until I'm completely submerged, bubble head of curlers and all.

When Rob returns with the coffee I'm still in the bath and have removed half of the curlers and bobby pins from my hair. I'm humming, but not committed to, "My Baby Just Cares for Me." Every once in a while I falter and start humming sounds that aren't related to any tune I know. I unwind a green plastic curler and chuck it into the garbage can.

Rob sets my coffee on the edge of the tub. "What now?"

I pause my humming long enough to say, "Fuck if I know."

Rob flinches—I have a way of making him do that, as if I'm causing him psychic pain. "You realize you didn't start swearing until this Nina Simone thing. That means you can stop."

"I don't want to stop, and I don't want to get out of the tub." I stare at the swells of my pale skin breaching the water, buoyant.

"You never let me see you anymore," he says. He's looking at the bathwater near my feet.

"Pardon me?" I say, having heard him clearly.

"I haven't seen you naked in three months."

"I just was. I am now."

Rob is still staring at the bathwater near my feet. He's shaking his head. "No, you know what I mean."

Before I can think about it I fling myself at him, sending waves of bathwater and suds over the edge of the tub. My coffee falls behind the toilet. I fly into his chest and wrap my arms around his neck, smashing my mouth against his. He struggles against me, tries to hold me away, but I heave myself against him until I've pushed him off the toilet. I'm falling on top of him, mouth open, ready to bite his lip, ready to grind my hips against his leg, when I hit my head on the corner of the vanity—a good, solid crack. I roll off him, my hand to my head. If he says a word, of either sympathy or mockery, I'll have to leave him. The bathroom is eerily quiet, except for the water sloshing in the tub. The cold tiles bite into my ass. What songs of our past will we sing to our children, or regale our friends with over dinner? Surely not this.

We don't say a word. He wraps me in a thick white towel and guides me to the bed. He fills one of his dress socks with ice from the machine and props it on my head. I fall asleep. He lets me.

I've packed only Nina clothes and Rob's packed only Mingus clothes, so we're stuck with the costumes.

"We should throw that gun in the ocean," he says.

"I don't think so," I say, pulling up my fresh stockings. "I think that's illegal."

Rob waits for me to finish dressing, which is taking too long because I don't want to wear the Nina clothes anymore. I'm tired and I don't want to go to the party. I step into the yellow dress and pull it up around me. I turn my back to Rob.

"Zip me." The dress is wrinkled now, and yellow doesn't suit my mood. How could I have worn such a tarty thing? "Unzip me."

"Here we go," says Rob. "I'll be in the bar."

After trying on everything in our suitcase, I end up wearing Rob's tuxedo pants and shirt and my red sandals. The shirt I've had to tie around me, it's so big, and the pants are held up by a patent-leather belt, but overall I look OK. Interesting and un-Nina-like. I spray myself with perfume, apply lipstick, shake my head to fluff my hair.

I pick up Rob in the bar, where a new bartender is on shift and there's no sign of Jerome or the woman my husband has plied with drink and talk of music. We continue down the Coast Highway. The air feels cool and wet, and my teeth are chattering, but I won't ask Rob to put the top up. It's late when we arrive—around eleven. The house is a sprawling glass-and-stucco compound. Palm trees wave and dip by the front door. I can't get beyond the whiteness of the ceramic-tiled room we're shown to, its multiple levels and glass walls with a view of the sea. All the women are naked. Not really, but they might as well be. Scraps of dresses cling to hips and hang off nipples. The women shimmer, metallic, as if wearing fish scales. Nothing I own would be appropriate here—not my Nina dresses, not the clothes I wear to work, and certainly not Rob's tuxedo pants and shirt.

Rob takes me by the elbow and pushes me toward a group of people. On the way I take a glass of champagne from the silver tray of a waitress. We are dressed surprisingly alike and I smile at her. She returns the smile, but when I glance back to see if she's held it, it's gone. She looks tired. At least she made an effort.

Our awkward progress is stopped when we run into our targeted group, the patrons Rob has gotten money from and wants to keep getting money from. We should have been here hours ago, but it doesn't matter. All these people are committed to giving a certain amount in the name of jazz, and the parties remind them that it feels good to give. Rob talks to these people a long time without introducing me. The host, an older man in a green turtleneck and dark gray slacks, makes eye contact with me several times during Rob's spiel about some technical aspect of a trumpet solo during a recent concert. Even I know this is dull. Finally, the host says, "Who's your friend, Rob?"

Rob bows slightly. "Pardon me. My wife, Alicia"—as if I'm some kind of trick or prize. I was once. The Junior League wanted me. Rob wanted me. I was full of glowing potential.

I shake the old guy's hand. "How's the food?"

The man keeps smiling but there's something behind the smile—an awareness that the question is strange, that the asker is, too. Before he can respond, a younger man with Gene Wilder hair holds up a china plate. He's chewing whatever his mouth is full of when he speaks.

"Food's OK," he says. "Mushroom, caviar, sour cream stuff. But the plates—"

He has cleaned his plate so thoroughly that when he holds it up for me it relinquishes neither a crumb nor a dribble of food. The plate catches the light from the candelabrum, its silver edges glimmering. The white china is so fine that even the faint light of the candles glows through until the plate looks like the full moon.

I look from the plate to the curly-haired man's face. He's still chewing, but he's nodding at me.

"Wow," I say. I move away from Rob and Mr. Moneybags. "Are you a musician?"

"Yup, Artie," he says, shaking my hand. "You?"

"Alicia, wife of Rob." I gesture to Rob with my head. "He raises money for the orchestra."

Artie snorts, shakes his head, and looks like he might say something complicated. "Let's get food."

Artie and I fill our plates with fresh strawberries and kiwi, little red potatoes with sour cream and caviar, mini mushroom turnovers, beautiful pink salmon draped across tidy beds of white rice, and mini cups of crème brûlée. I glance at Rob, who continues to chat up the man in the green turtleneck. Artie and I make our way through the glass doors, to the porch. The wind whips my hair.

"Come on," Artie says, and he's about to lead me down the plank steps to the sand when he says, "No, wait." He hands me his plate and runs inside, disappearing around a corner. I smell the sea, and the salt makes my mouth water. Artie returns with several afghans thrown over his right arm; in the other hand he manages a bottle of champagne and two glasses.

"Good hands," I say.

"You know what they say about trumpet players."

"Good embouchure?"

We walk a short way down the beach until we find some dunes that offer shelter from the wind. We spread one afghan on the sand and wrap ourselves in the other two. I feel spiteful for walking out on Rob, but I remind myself I am only getting a bite to eat. While we eat we talk only of the food. When we've finished, Artie stretches out on the afghan. Through the open doors we can hear the music, but none of the crowd noise comes through.

"Best seat in the house," Artie says.

I'm sitting up, hugging my knees, facing the ocean. For the moment, I feel content. "If you could do anything you wanted, what would you do?"

"Play the best music with the best musicians in the world," he says, without hesitating.

"Aren't you doing that?"

"It's hard to say. There may be some cat in Japan who's the best bassist, or some chick in Qatar who can ululate like nobody's business." He turns to look at me. "What about you?"

I don't try to answer seriously—I say the first thing that pops into my head. "I want to live in the ocean, and catch little fish in my open mouth."

"Have you been to Japan?" Artie asks.

"I wish I could say yes, but no."

"Can't find fresher fish."

Artie, I realize, has been all over the world. "What do you do Saturday mornings?"

"Stay in bed. When I'm so hungry I have to get up, I walk to the bakery. If it's nice, I sit outside and watch people. Then I go home and listen to music."

"What books do you read?"

"Short ones. I hate to be interrupted. The moon—my God, have you ever seen such a thing?"

"Every night."

He brushes my leg with the back of his hand. "Who's that corpse you're with? And why doesn't he care that you're with me?"

"That corpse makes sure you get paid."

"Fuck that. Is that what he tells you? When rich people give money for jazz they feel smart and holy and pure. It has nothing to do with him."

I wonder if this is true, and I feel sad for Rob. I wish Artie had not met me this way. I hold one of the plates between me and the moon.

"I wonder if the moon will show through."

Artie shakes his head. "Come on. It's just a plate."

We're quiet a while.

"We should sleep together someday," he says.

"Someday sounds possible." Why not now, is what I'm thinking.

Instead, I keep asking Artie questions: Best New Year's Eve. Favorite color. Number of women slept with. Place in order of importance: Food, Sex, Music, Sleep. Color of hair as a baby. He lets me touch his hair.

"Don't cut it," I say.

"Women hate my hair."

"Fuck them. I love it."

More questions: Favorite baseball team. Best memory of a summer day from childhood. Favorite childhood book. Painted toenails—yes or no?

"Saturday morning in bed—what are you doing?"

"Staring. Feeling the edge of the blanket between my thumb and fingers. Listening to the leaves, the birds, the ceiling fan."

"Best part of sex?"

"Kissing."

Artie has had his eyes closed for the last ten minutes or so but he has answered my questions. Now his hair flutters around his eyelids. I touch his nose, his cheek. I kiss his trumpet-player lips and he kisses back, a sleepy instinct. The inside of his mouth tastes like pot roast. I wonder, what does the inside of his trumpet smell like? It would be frightfully easy to sleep with him. I imagine waking up Saturday mornings, both of us listening to the sounds of his room and the outdoors. Over breakfast we'd watch the people passing the café. Later, we would read and listen to music. Maybe I'd go to Artie's concert; maybe I'd stay home or go out with friends. Then we'd get up Sunday and do it all over again. During the week I'd tell him about the people I'd seen at the museum. He'd go away on tours, and we'd talk nights or, more likely, afternoons, on the phone.

I pull the afghan around me, covering my head, but the wind is too cold. How does anyone enjoy the exaggerated drama of the California coast? The stinging spray of the icy water, the slashing wind, the sharp rocks—it makes a pretty picture, but what a waste of shoreline, beach, and surf. I shiver. Artie would go to parties like this one without me all the time, unless I went with him everywhere, following him around like a tin can or an old shoe tied to the bumper of a car.

I leave him dozing on the beach and take our plates down to the freezing water to rinse them. I hurry down the beach toward the music. I see a tall figure on the deck, and I know it's Rob. I run toward him. When he turns, he's smiling. But his turning reveals a Young Bene-factress in a green silk sheath with a glossy up-do. Rob leans over the deck rail. "Hey, lady. Where've you been?"

I decide to play it straight. Hell, I don't have to play it any way. He's *my* husband. "I ate dinner with Artie, the trumpet player. I decided not to fuck him."

Rob flinches. The Green-Sheathed Benefactress smiles, red-lipped, and glides away.

"Glad to hear it," Rob says, and I'm almost sorry I've said it. "What have you got there?"

"Plates. I'm going to shoot them up. Watch."

I dig inside my purse for the Taurus. This is not the proper use for the .38 Special, as described to me by the man at the pawnshop. It's meant for personal protection, not skeet. It's an impossible task, to explode china plates with a .38 as they fly through the air. I have to try, though.

Rob clumps down the steps rather quickly, by the sound of it. I point the gun at him.

"Stay there."

He stops at the bottom of the steps.

"Watch."

It's much harder to pull the trigger on this type of gun than most people realize. To accidentally shoot my husband I would have to stumble, or be bashed on the head with something heavy and have an electrical reaction, some kind of biological reflex.

"I'm watching." He seems not the slightest bit nervous that I am pointing a loaded gun at him. I wonder if people who deserve to be shot are often taken by surprise when they finally are.

I turn to the task at hand—damaging our host's fine china. I throw one plate and sure enough, Artie was right—there's no lunar translucence. I fire at the plate when it seems hung up in the black sky. I miss. The plate makes a hollow thunk on the sand, landing perfectly flat and ready for the next course. I throw the other plate as hard as I can, getting my whole body into it so that when I fire, I do so without aiming and I miss. This one lands funny, breaks. I race to the other plate and I'm getting ready to hurl it to the sky when I feel Rob behind me. He grabs me around my middle, presses his front into my back. He grips my wrist. Many people have gathered on the deck. I see the flicker of their colorful gowns, hear the low murmur of voices. Rob takes the plate.

"Alicia," he says. I relax against him and turn to lay my head on his chest. He steps away. "Let me."

I watch him as he reels back, uncoils himself, and flings the plate into the sky with a grunt. I forget to watch the plate in its soaring arc. I watch Rob instead. The tail of his silk shirt flaps in the wind. He stands with his hands on his hips, watching the arc of the white plate. When it starts to drop, he looks at me and says, "What are you waiting for? Shoot!"

His face is pale, and his eyebrows make the perfect parentheses of surprise seen on riders of roller coasters, when their photos are snapped at the initial moment of descent from the coaster's highest point.

The pistol seems too heavy to hold. I point the gun away from us, somewhere in the direction of the falling plate, and squeeze the trigger. The man in the green turtleneck, who owns this house, this deck, this strip of beach, speaks to us from his deck.

"As long as no one gets hurt . . . I do have neighbors—"

One of his guests responds, "Harvey, I thought you bought the neighbors!"

The guests laugh. The man in the green turtleneck seems worried for our safety or the safety of his neighbors. Maybe he's just worried about lawsuits and wrongful death, but there's a note of concern in his voice. There is a sense of limit, which I badly need.

Rob runs to where the plate has landed, outside the pool of light shining from the deck. He yells over his shoulder at me, "You missed. Let's go again."

The plate has a smile-shaped portion missing from its edge, as if someone has taken a bite out of it. He holds it like a Frisbee.

"Ready?"

The gun hangs at my side. I don't have the strength to lift it.

"It won't work."

"Try," he says, as if everything depends on it.

The people on the deck watch us. Some of them clap, the way they might after a particularly good performance when they are hoping for an encore—something, anything, to keep them from having to squint into the house lights and head home. While I'm hesitating, the Young Benefactress, sheathed in satin, wobbles down the plank steps in her high heels. She beams at Rob, reaching toward the pistol in my hand. I feel her hand softly on mine. Her face is so pale, her cheekbones high like glowing moons.

She turns to me, her eyes shining. "I want to try. Can I?"

I let go of the gun. I don't wait to see how she does. Inside, I find a phone in an office, far down a dim hallway. In California, it can't be unusual for a woman with no luggage, wearing a man's tuxedo, to need a cab to the airport well past midnight. Palms tick outside in the breeze. The sound of the gun firing doesn't sound like a gun firing when someone else pulls the trigger. Quiet notes drift from the living room. Disconnected from one another, they fall in my ear, pearls.

Tiger

Tiger and I roll in to Tiffany & Co., hunting for a sterling silver choker. Tiger pauses to sniff the chilled air, then trots over to a customer in a purple silk dress. Her back is turned. Tiger's loud purr rumbles, and he bumps his nose into the woman's backside, licking and sniffing. The woman stiffens. Then she bends forward, allowing Tiger deeper access, but he's already lost interest. Turning away, he licks his nose and pads back to me at the counter.

"I'd like a collar," I say to the clerk.

His reddish-blond hair is swept away from his face. His cheeks are somewhat hollow. He smirks at me. "For your tiger?"

I place my hand on Tiger's neck and work my fingers into his thick fur.

"No," I say, "for me."

The clerk guides me away from the silver I favor and snares me with a delicate three-strand gold-link choker. Each link of the center strand holds a diamond.

"The gold suits your blond hair and pale skin," the man says. "More so than the silver."

I hold it up around my neck.

"And you're so petite," he continues. "Whatever you wear should be delicate, gossamer—"

"Like tiffany?" I say.

"Yes," he says, smirking again, as if every young woman who comes here makes that joke. "Like tiffany."

I finger the fragile links. It is lovely, but I know better. I'll need something stronger—something I can really feel. Tiger and I settle on a choker of heavy silver links, with a big tennis ball charm, which hangs to the center of my chest.

"Tiger likes to play with tennis balls," I explain. Tiger licks his lips.

The man ignores my explanation, as if to say women who shop at Tiffany & Co. do not lower themselves to explain their purchases, their pets, or anything.

"Would you like that engraved?"

I glance at Tiger. He looks away.

"No, thank you."

The clerk places the necklace on a rectangle of cotton batting in the glossy blue box.

"Wait," I say. "Would you—?"

He comes from behind the counter to fasten the necklace around me. I feel the mistake of it—the silver so heavy and dull. The man is close; his cologne stinks. Tiger purrs and flicks his tail.

"You have what you want, madam?"

I believe the clerk disapproves of my choice, and I would like, in this moment, for the clerk to tell me what I want. Tell me what I want and let me have it. He wears cowboy boots, made from some reptile. I finger the choker and stare at the pointed toes of his shoes.

"Alligator," he says. "I killed it myself."

I imagine him topless, barrel-chested and waist deep in a Florida swamp, wrestling a pale-bellied gator. I lean in to sniff his teeth: ham, peppercorn, vinegar.

"I'll scruff you," I say.

"You'll do no such thing," he says.

Tiger watches; his purring has quieted.

"I'll whack your nose," I say to the man.

He folds his arms, laughs, leans back against the counter.

Tiger saunters in the direction of the purple-dress woman. I hear her murmur of delight when he greets her lap with his moist nose.

The man reaches out to pluck the dull charm from my chest. It disappears in his hand. He pulls me closer and locks his eyes on mine. I won't look away. I grab his cowboy hair at the base of his neck.

"Grrr," he says.

"Grrr yourself," I say, and we circle and circle.

Glen Echo

Happier times: The summer before I proposed, the summer Gina and I met. I played at being a badass, and after sixteen hours of coiling cable and loading and unloading lighting kits, I rode my motorcycle from Baltimore to Rockville for a party. I swaggered in, said "Hey, babe" to the hostess—a high school girlfriend of mine—and grabbed a beer from the cooler in the back. Gina was there, looking petite and fiery, her skinny arms so dark from the sun and her eyes wide almonds. I took a swig of beer and realized she was the only woman on the patio I hadn't slept with. She caught me looking at her. I walked up and said, "I want you." She smirked and tossed her hair like a wild horse that would sooner kick my teeth in than nuzzle my neck. I followed her inside and kept close at her back, whispering all the things I could do for her. The thing is, she let me. She stopped at a big plastic bowl of shrimp, peeled one and swirled it around in the cocktail sauce while I told her about stroking her back, kissing her shoulders, and biting her neck. Then I told her some shit about buying her a house and making her my queen and how I'd bow down before her every night when I came home from work. She turned to me and said, "You're crazy." She was so close I could almost feel her small round breasts on my arm. Her boyfriend, a clean-cut guy, approached and introduced himself. He was obviously nice. I groaned. I hated to do it.

"I want to fuck your girlfriend," I said.

"That's nice," he said, and the two of them left the party.

It took me about a week to track Gina down through mutual friends. I convinced her there would be no harm in dating me while continuing her relationship with her boyfriend. Try me out, I said. If you don't like me, forget I exist, and the boyfriend's none the wiser. Within two days, I had Gina at Glen Echo Park. I gave her a tour of the grounds, as if I were a king and the park my kingdom. As if to say, All this for you, my Queen: the dilapidated Spanish Ballroom with the springy wood floor and floor-to-ceiling windows; the deserted bumper-car pavilion, ghosts of all the spatially challenged nerd-kids stuck in the corners; and the empty Crystal Pool with its blue-painted bottom. We scuffed past the low arcade with its peeling paint, and I told her the history of the place—about all the families and young couples who'd had fun here before the park had closed. From the rear of the puppet theater came the smell of sour paint. At the merry-go-round I lifted her onto a big white horse with a chipped plaster mane and I kissed the inside of her thighs. I told her we'd be married someday and I'd do things like this to her every day—twice a day—in the morning and at night.

Here's how it is now: I've got my head up the skirt of Gina's wedding gown. It's garter-toss time. I'm supposed to be locating the garter but I can't find anything under here, amid all these layers of frothy white. Are there even legs in here? Help me out, Gina. At first the crowd of coworkers, friends, and assorted family members thought it amusing that I couldn't find my way around my wife's nether region. There was much snorting and laughing, which I could hear, muffled by yards and yards of whatever this itchy white shit is called. Tool? That's how you say it. Now it's quiet, though, and I can hear our guests thinking "Incompetent." "Nitwit." "Stupid ass."

Finally, Gina finds my hand underneath the layers of skirt and places it directly on the garter. I can hear her thinking, "Dickhead," but more accurately what I'm feeling is "Ineffectual." I slide it down her calf and over her shoe. I emerge from her skirt and wave the garter over my head. The crowd hoots and claps. Gina leans back in the chair, her elbows up on the back of it, her legs spread like a cowboy. I'm not sure what these gestures mean. Maybe she's too tired to keep her knees together. Maybe she's drunk.

Let me back up: At dinner, my new wife, who has been unable to eat anything but oatmeal for three days because of nerves, tucks her napkin into the neck of her gown, picks up her fork, and doesn't look up until her plate is clean. I'm not kidding: the rubbery chicken, the shriveled string beans, the potatoes with incinerated onions, the roll with the pat of butter. Every time I look at her, her cheeks are popped out, full of food. I've never—never—seen her eat this way. I talk politely to her friend Carrie—a very skinny person—who, as maid of honor, sits to my right. I glance over once in a while to see if she's slowed down any, but she's still going strong. When she's mopping her plate with the dinner roll and reaching over for mine, I suggest we visit with our guests. She looks at me like I'm crazy, and moves the chunk of food to her left cheek so she can reply: "I'm eating."

When the DJ announces the first dance, I'm tapping my chocolate dessert cup with my spoon while she breaks off bits of hers and dips it into the raspberry mousse it contains. I fear she'll refuse the dance, standing up to yell "I'm eating," but instead she takes the napkin from the neck of her gown and stands. She holds out her hand and waggles her fingers at me to hurry up. Gina walks us quickly to the center of the floor and has herself in position before the music starts. Now, whenever I've been to weddings, during the first dance the happy couple look at each other, they talk a little, rub noses, laugh tenderly—they act like they like each other. Not us, not today, not during our first dance as husband and wife. Gina looks over my shoulder the whole time. No eye contact—none.

Happier times, part two: When I worked sixteen-hour calls in Baltimore, Gina would drive all the way from her parents' house in Rockville with my dinner. She always wore some piece of my clothing, usually something only I would notice—maybe the elastic of my boxers would peek from the waistband of her jeans, or one of my earrings would dangle from her lobe. Once, she showed up wearing a pair of my old leather driving gloves—the fingerless kind—and that knocked me out. My legs were a little quivery after these visits. Sometimes I'd pretend to walk Gina back to her car, my hand on her lower back, and I'd guide her to the rear of the concession stand and try to devour her.

Earlier on our wedding day: When we arrive at the reception site, Gina disappears with her cousin Lou and Carrie. Apparently, the yards and yards of dress make it impossible to go to the bathroom solo. As they walk by, Lou flashes me a big smile with those red, red lips of hers, but I don't take it personally. She's all of nineteen, and she smiles that way at everyone. Gina appears stony and preoccupied—the usual for her lately. Lou finds some reason to laugh, and the silvery chimes of her voice set off tones up and down my spine. We have some history, which she probably doesn't remember, which I'm a bastard for thinking of on my wedding day.

I wait in the cocktail area, holding a cube of cheese between my thumb and forefinger. No one will talk to me. I feel stupid for having to stand alone at a big party even after I've gotten married. Across the fake oriental carpet, my father strides toward me. My face goes mushy—a happy-sad swirl of confusion. My heart swells at the sight of his gray mullet. With his cowboy boots, the tux looks lived-in, real. This is how a man dresses. Have I learned nothing?

"Son," he says.

"Dad," I say, and what I mean is "help."

He gives careful instructions. "I left your helmet with the bike. Here are your keys—in case you need to make a quick getaway."

I hadn't thought of this. I imagine peeling out of the parking lot, gunning the engine until Gina's people cover their ears with their hands. They're mouthing words like "asshole," "bum," and "motherfucker," but I can't hear them. I feel a stab of guilt, so in my fantasy, I plunk Gina down behind me on the Harley. The bike skids and slides out from under us: we wreck.

Dad grips my hand and says, "Seriously. Get yourself a drink. Stay a while. I'll take the bike home at the end of the night, if Gina has other ideas."

He draws himself up and pulls his glasses from his pocket. He scans the room. I realize Gina will always have other ideas, and that I am standing next to a man who has been married for three decades to a woman with a few of her own. He could have told me, but he didn't. "Where is that woman?" he mutters. "Have you seen your mother?" We wander off separately, looking for our other halves.

I head down the hallway where I last saw my bride. I find her around the corner, by herself except for her eight-year-old nephew, Frank. For a second, I'm disappointed that Lou is gone. Frank is responsible for making the "Just Married" sign on the back of the limo, except he left out the "i" and instead the sign reads, "Just Marred." When we were leaving St. Martin's, Gina saw the sign and said, "Fucking-A." The priest pretended not to hear. Now she has her hand on the back of Frank's head and she's pushing his face into the wall, pinning him. In her other hand, she's holding up a portion of the frou-frou skirt of her dress. A wad of gray chewing gum is stuck in it. I must have startled her because she loses her grip on Frank, and he runs off. "Hey, you little fucker!" she yells, and she reaches below her dress, pulls off a white satin shoe and hurls it at the retreating Frank. She clocks him in the back of the head, and the heel makes a loud thunk when it connects. "Jesus, not the head," I say. Gina whips off her other shoe and hurls it, but Frank turns the corner and the shoe hits a large peach and turquoise print of an iris or a sunset, I can't tell which.

"That little shit—" Gina says.

Before she can finish, I have gotten my knife out of my pocket. I cut the offending gum out of the foamy skirt of her gown. She punches me in the chest. "What are you doing?"

I wad up the small square and put it in my pants pocket along with my knife. Then I floof up the netting of her skirt. That's when I realize how huge this thing really is. "Look," I say. "You can't even tell a piece is missing."

Gina concedes the point, I guess, because all she says is "Isn't this the cocktail hour?"

Gina has this thing planned to the minute. If it were up to me we'd be knee-deep in the Crystal Pool at Glen Echo Park, splashing with our friends and family, lining up for fried chicken and coleslaw, but Gina wouldn't have it. She didn't take me seriously, probably because the park closed in the '60s. The merry-go-round still runs—it even has a tarnished brass ring—and the puppet theater operates during the summer. Artists rent out little studios in the park, and you can watch them paint or make wooden bowls or whatever it is they do. I go there a lot to look at the abandoned amusements. I like to fantasize that we could get all the rides running again—fill the Crystal Pool and polish the slides, grease the bumper cars, have a big dance party in the Spanish Ballroom. Instead we're in Ballroom A at the Holiday Inn, and our honeymoon suite has a jacuzzi tub with scummy white tiles. The brochure the Holiday Inn planner gave us claims the hotel specializes in "dream weddings." The picture on the front features a guy dressed in tails sitting at a piano, serenading a pair of "Just Marreds." I thought the guy was Bing Crosby for about three months. That was why I agreed to the Holiday Inn—not because I thought Bing Crosby would have anything to do with our wedding, but I thought, OK, well, this adds something. It reminded me of that old movie *Holiday Inn*, which is what the Holiday Inn people want you to think about. When I looked more closely at the photo one day after Gina and I had spent five hours addressing invitations, I realized that the guy was definitely not Bing Crosby and that the photo had been faked—made to look old and charming and of bygone days. The hotel people made no effort, it seemed to me, in the actual hotel, to attain any kind of old-fashioned charm or nostalgia.

In the burgundy foyer where we're having cocktails, Gina inspects the trays. We've skimped here. We've done only two, a cheese and a veggie—just enough to keep people from getting shit-faced before dinner. One of Gina's weird friends from high school wants us to open her present. I try to get us out of it while Gina stands there.

"We're waiting until after the honeymoon," I say.

"It's my original art," the woman says. "I like to see people's reaction."

The woman—Anya is her name—wears earrings made from cockroaches encased in Lucite. It's all I can focus on. I can't hear her speaking anymore, and everything around us has gone dark. Finally, Gina yanks on my finger so hard it pulls out of joint. We're moving toward the gift table, which is inside the hall. Gina looks serene. She brushes a stray wisp of hair from her face and smoothes the front of her gown. I've seen this before. It's the calm before the bitch.

I stand behind her as she opens the present, which is wrapped in brown paper and tied with twine. "I like what you've done with the wrapping," I say. Gina elbows me. Inside the wrapping is a mirror, about the size of an 8 x 10 photo. I see us—me and Gina—reflected. Me standing over Gina's shoulder, our newlywed faces framed by a border of gleaming Lucite-encrusted cockroaches. Gina's face looks deadly calm. "It's your cockroach thing," she says.

"They're palmetto bugs," Anya says. "They fly."

"Not anymore," I say.

Gina puts the mirror on the gift table. While the two of them say good-bye, I cover it with the brown paper.

We watch Anya leave. As soon as the door shuts behind her, Gina whirls to the table and snatches up the mirror. She marches off toward the kitchen, and I stumble after her. We sweep in so quickly no one has a chance to respond. Gina's veil floats behind her, twitching and jerking as she motors toward the exit. I'm worried, for some reason, about the hem of her dress, which I've already stepped on countless times. It will get dirty—it's already dirty—and there's nothing I can do about it. In the alley, she hurls the mirror against the brick wall of the hotel. It doesn't shatter. She stomps on it with her heels. That does it. She lets me take her in my arms. "Why do people have to be so weird?" She clutches the lapels of my jacket.

"Shh, shh," I say.

She pulls away, again smoothing the front of her dress. She wipes the hair and tears from her face and sighs. "We'd better get back," she says, and she hikes up her gown, stepping past me to the concrete stairs leading back to the kitchen. I forget to offer her my arm or my elbow or something of use, but she doesn't seem to need it anyway. I follow the white netting, aware of the ache in my knees. How long can this last? I've been awake too long today, and in general, haven't been getting enough sleep. I want this to be over, so Gina and I can get back to our normal lives—if we can remember what that was like.

Nothing has been normal since I proposed to Gina at my parents' house on Super Bowl Sunday. I had a ring for her, but not *the* ring because I knew she'd want to pick that out herself. This was a "promise ring," the clerk at Zales told me. Not a diamond-chip ring either, where you have to close one eye and squint the other to see the sparkle. This ring had a big sapphire in it—with a diamond chip on either side. I had Gina in the bathroom. She had gone upstairs because the downstairs bathroom is right off the TV room and you can hear everything. I barged in after her.

"Get out," she said, pushing against my chest. "I have to pee."

I sat on the vanity, next to the sink. "So go," I told her.

"You're such a child," she said.

"But that's what you love about me," I said.

She smiled at me from the toilet. I always get her.

"Do you do this at work, Randy? Follow ladies into the restroom to watch them pee? Is that what you like, kink-boy?"

I blushed. Gina always gets me, too. She washed her hands at the sink, and when she finished, she turned off the tap and flicked water in my face. "Your parents know you watch girls pee?"

I blocked the door. "Listen," I said, "I don't know why I'm asking you this now but it seems like the right time." I pulled the velvet-covered box out of my front pocket and held it up to her face. "You want to marry me?"

She looked at me, her brown eyes perfectly calm, her curly dark hair a wild mane.

"Just say yes," I said. "That's what you're supposed to say."

She took the box, but didn't open it right away. Instead she sat on the toilet and fingered the blue velvet.

"That's not *the* ring," I told her. "Just something to wear until you pick out what you want."

She looked up. "A promise ring," she said.

She still hadn't opened the box, and I was getting nervous. I hadn't imagined so much discussion. I had imagined Gina flinging herself at me as soon as I produced the box, because "ring box" means "proposal," after all.

Gina crossed her legs and squinted up at me. "So, what do you promise, Randy? What comes with the ring?"

I thought she was playing with me. "You get me, babe. Forever."

She opened the box. That sapphire really sparkled, thanks to the spotlight over the toilet. Gina took the ring out and said, "When?"

"Are you saying yes, or are you saying maybe—it depends on the date?"

"I'm saying 'When?'"

I shrugged. "Anytime. Now. Tomorrow. Next weekend."

She put the ring back in the box.

"Wait a minute, what's wrong? What time's better than the present?"

"That's not enough time," she said, "for the kind of wedding I want."

Gina wanted a traditional wedding, she said. I'd never thought of her as being traditional, what with all the premarital sex and cohabitation, and I wasn't sure what that meant, but it was what she wanted so I nodded. We hammered out a few preliminaries there in my parents' second-floor bathroom and then went downstairs to announce the news.

All of what I had to offer, it turned out, could rightly fall under the category "How Far Can Randy Be Pushed?" or maybe "What Randy Will Tolerate."

First, we stopped having sex. Not entirely, but she seemed preoccupied. She jumped out of bed in the morning, showered and dressed and made coffee while I slept, dreaming of molesting her under the covers. Then I'd reach for her. No Gina. I'd wake up to hear her keys rattling in the door, the car starting in the drive: Gina off to try on dresses, taste cake, fight with her mother about who should or should not be a bridesmaid. She'd return, exhausted and cranky.

"Why are you doing this to yourself?" I'd ask. I was thinking, "Why are you doing this to us?" and "Where have all the good times gone?"

Next, she took me around to meet all her relatives. We had trips planned every weekend: New Jersey, New York, Connecticut. I shook hands with uncles and aunts who seemed to have their minds made up about me when we drove up on my bike. All suspicion was erased when Gina ticked off the details of our wedding over coffee and Stella D'Oro cookies. We were doing it right, as far as they were concerned. I couldn't be all bad, even if I did have a ponytail and a Harley. I saw the way those women looked at me. I knew what they were thinking: It won't be long before that hair is gone—and the bike, too.

I met Frank on one of these trips. I put Gina's helmet on him—it was too big—and rode him around the block a few times. He seemed like a good kid. For the rest of the day he wouldn't take the helmet off. "Frank," I said, kneeling down, right before we had to leave, "if you don't give it back, we'll get arrested." His eyes got all big. "On the Tappan Zee, the cops will stop us. You don't want your Cousin Gina to get arrested, do you?" He said, very quietly, "You're a liar." Then he ran off. I laughed about it then, but I'm pretty sure he's right—I am a liar and worse.

In addition to the road trips, Gina's female relatives began dropping in for days at a time to help "plan." Bridesmaids' dresses had to be selected, then rejected. Jordan almonds, pastries, and Italian cream cakes had to be ordered. The women descended on our little house with their cosmetic bags and their fingernails and their jewelry, and they whisked Gina away for hours at a time, never asking if I'd like to join them or if I had an opinion about Jordan almonds, cream cakes—or bridesmaids' dresses, for that matter. As far as they were concerned, my wedding had nothing to do with me.

Have I mentioned the size of the wedding party? Gina's side consists of her two best friends from middle school, four friends from college, three friends from work, three cousins (including Lou), and the daughter of her father's business partner.

"Thirteen bridesmaids," I said, when she told me. "Isn't that unlucky?"

Gina gave me a disgusted look, as if I were the biggest idiot in the world. I was getting used to this and was beginning to think that I was, probably, the biggest idiot in the world.

"Nine bridesmaids," she said. "Three junior bridesmaids, and one flower girl."

My side consisted of my best man—my father—and Frank, the ring-bearer. The only guy I could think to stand up for me was my best friend from middle school, Charles, but I stopped by his mother's house on Eutaw Street and she said he's been living in Alaska for the past two years. I thought about asking one of my female friends—an ex—but I knew Gina would tell me to go fuck myself, right before she brought some heavy object down on my head. She filled out the rest of my side with her brothers and cousins and nephews.

Two months before the wedding, Lou came to stay with us in Rockville. For once, this wasn't a visit related to wedding prep; Lou was visiting colleges in D.C. Louise is her name, but no one except her mother calls her that. She planned to major in music, and she had some soprano. For a week I listened to her singing in the bathroom, and not just when she showered in the morning. Whenever she had a spare minute she would lock herself in there and partake of the acoustics. What made it so uncomfortable for me was that the bathroom had two doors: one that led to the hallway and one that led to our bedroom. So in the morning, it was like a concert all for me. I didn't really like her style—too diva, too Mariah Carey–Whitney Houston. Good pipes, but a lot of wailing and fussiness, to the point where sometimes I couldn't even pick out the melody. But I have to admit, I was getting used to waking up to the sound of her voice. I lay there and thought about the flimsy things between us: the white sheet covering me, the three feet of air between the bed and the bathroom, the hollow-core door, which I could put my fist through, if I wanted. Did she stand or sit? Take her clothes off or leave them on? The first couple mornings I jumped out of bed, feeling I was invading her privacy. By the third day I was rolling over, pulling the pillow over my head, trying to black out visions of Lou in her high heels and nothing else, singing her brains out.

I was in charge of driving her to her appointments at the colleges and universities she wanted to attend. While she was visiting, her father rented a white Lincoln Continental for me to drive her around in. I guess he didn't like the idea of his daughter straddling my Harley and wrapping her arms around me. When she wasn't singing in the bathroom, preparing for her auditions, Lou tended her manicure on the sofa in the living room. She had fire-engine-red talons, and she was always brushing clear goop over them, blowing on her fingers and singing to them.

"You'll give yourself brain damage," I said. "That stuff stinks."

Lou laughed at my little joke. She had big curly hair—reddish—and she wore red lipstick, all the time, to match her nails. Did I mention she laughed at my jokes?

I waited outside during her interviews and auditions. Usually I read the bulletin boards announcing scholarships and temporary jobs for musicians: page-turner, accompanist, piano player at Nordstrom's. Some life. I wondered what Lou would do. Marry some guy, have babies, sing to them.

The idea of Lou marrying herself off rapidly after college, ruining her life and possibly someone else's, depressed me. I thought about Lou going through four or five years of school, singing her heart out, polishing her nails to a high gloss, and then marrying some fat opera singer and having his babies. Instead, I wanted to pick Gina up after work and drive to the Kennedy Center to watch Lou on stage—single and buxom with her vibrant red nails, about to be murdered by Pagliaccio, or beheaded by Elizabeth I. I fantasized about carrying Lou's sheet music, bringing her glasses of water at rehearsals, following along with the music as she practiced, her every note raising the hairs on the back of my neck. As a result of these fantasies, in Lou's presence my skin prickled and itched, as if my cells were trying to abandon me for her.

On the way back from her last audition, I begged her to sing me some opera.

"I don't know any opera," she said.

"How can you be a singer and not know any opera? Isn't that, like, what you aspire to?"

She sang a medley of Motown tunes instead. I interrupted her.

"Too many notes," I said.

"Are you counting?"

"I'm just saying, you're making it too fancy."

I kept berating her but she never got mad, so I kept driving and before I knew where we were headed we were pulling into the parking lot at Glen Echo, all the abandoned rides and artists' studios lurking in front of us in the dusk. I took her to dinner at the inn there—told her to order whatever she wanted. I asked if she liked wine. She hesitated, looking guarded for a moment, then said, "Sure." We finished a bottle of Chianti and she ordered dessert, too. I could see that Lou would be zaftig someday, but now she was just right—biggish womanly breasts, hips, and thighs.

I hopped the fence into the park, then helped her over. She fell into my arms, a pillow of perfumed flesh. She was drunk. She asked for a cigarette when I lit one for myself.

"No way," I said. "Singers don't smoke."

She whined and hung all over me, trying to grab the cigarette from my hand. I enjoyed this for a while before lighting her one of her own.

I led her to the top of one of the artists' studios. Built into the side of little hills, they look like hobbit holes, but that's not what they're called. Dearths? No, but something that sounds like "dearth." We sat on top of one, dangling our legs over the doorway. She dropped one of her pointy white shoes.

"So," I said. "You're serious about this music thing?" Again, the fantasy of life with Lou loomed.

She giggled and tried to rest her head on my shoulder.

I shrugged her away. "I'm serious. What do you want from life?"

She gave me a surprisingly sober look. Her eyes were a watery brown, like root beer in a glass after all the ice has melted.

"I want what you and Gina have," she said.

I looked up at the black sky and the little pinprick stars.

"And what is it you think we have?"

She looked at me like I was the biggest fool. It must run in the family. There must be genetic code for that look.

"Companionship?" she said. "Love? Friendship?"

I nodded impatiently. "OK, fine. But what about your career? Your music? I mean, why have I been driving you all over Washington? So you can meet some fat chorus member and get knocked up?"

Her face went red, and she looked down, muttered something I couldn't hear.

"What? What did you say?"

"I could have taken the bus," she said. "You didn't have to drive me."

"You're missing the point," I said.

I drove us home, and she threw up out the window twice. The next morning there was a pinkish stain on the passenger door of the Connie.

Bouquet-toss time: All the single women stand at the back edge of the dance floor, as if they want everyone to believe that they don't believe in the magic of the bridal bouquet, or as I see it, the contagion of marriage transmitted by floral arrangement. Lou is among them, and so is Frank, until his father drags him away and swats the back of his head. Frank finds his way to my side.

"Am I still a liar?" I ask.

"What do you think?" he says. He sounds just like his mother, or any of the other female relatives, and I know that's where he's learned this phrase, along with the disdain.

"Let me buy you a drink," I say.

"I'm eight," Frank says.

I should be making an effort with the men, but I've resisted this so far. I'm on the verge of being disliked, and I can do something about it—mingle—or I can hang here with Frank.

"Frank," I say, "You're a first-class pussy."

"Takes one to know one, fucker," he says.

He's right. If I'd known about all this before I proposed, Gina and I would still be sleeping in on Saturdays, having breakfast in bed, and fooling around until noon. I wouldn't have to feel so bad for sort of disliking her—now at this late stage, when we've pledged our lives to each other—and I wouldn't be tied up in knots over Lou. But here we are on this stupid day when everything that goes wrong or right means something. At least I think it's supposed to.

Lou has brought her fat singer boyfriend, who, by the way, can really sing. He has a meaty-sounding tenor and none of Lou's vocal fussiness. He sang "Ave Maria" before the ceremony, and I wanted to marry him instead of Gina. My feet feel ready to break. In fact, they may have already, nothing but too-small rental shoes holding them together. That and a pair of damp dress socks.

Gina turns her back to the women and heaves the bouquet over her shoulder. It sails over their heads and hits a waiter in the chest—a do-over. She overcompensates on the second throw, and the bouquet falls short. It hits the parquet dance floor, and for a second nobody moves. Then Lou shoves her way from the back of the crowd and throws herself on it as if it's a grenade and she's sacrificing herself to save the others. Her bare arms slap the floor and her dress slides up, exposing her white knees and big thighs. She rises to her knees and holds the bouquet above her head in victory, then picks her boyfriend out of the crowd and shakes it at him. He claps as he walks over, then he plants a big kiss on her mouth. The crowd hoots and hollers, and people tap their spoons on their glasses.

I go to Gina's side. She clutches a glass of white wine.

"Throw the garter," she says.

The men assemble and more or less let Lou's big boyfriend have the garter. I wonder if there's any way I can miss this—Lou's transformation from Interesting Person with a Future to Bride with a capital *B*. I grab Gina's hand and say, "Let's go."

She doesn't protest. Her hand feels like a little bird in mine. On the way out, I take a bottle of champagne from the waiter who was struck by the bouquet. We walk quickly through the lobby to the parking lot. Someone has tied pink and white balloons to the back of the limo. Frank's sign declares us "Just Marred," and I imagine us wheeling off to our honeymoon on gurneys, wrapped in gauze, reaching out to grasp each other's broken limbs. The driver holds the door for us. I hesitate, and I pull Gina away from the dim interior of the limo.

"We're done with this," I say to the driver, to Gina. I give the man three twenties and ask him to drop our luggage at the hotel. I lead Gina past the limousine to my bike. When I offer her the helmet, she waves it away; she's still wearing her veil. She gathers up her gown, straddles the seat behind me, and stuffs the fabric between us. She doesn't ask where we're going.

On the way to Glen Echo, the other drivers honk at us. What must they think? Fun-loving couple, their lives ahead of them. With the big cushion of dress between us, I can barely feel Gina. At the red light at MacArthur, she takes the flowers, pins, and combs from her hair and flings them into the road. She slings her veil to the curb, and it lies there like a thing violated. At the next light, she hurls her shoes into the woods, making little grunts of exertion. I take off my bow tie, flick it to the ground, and unbutton my shirt. Sometime before we reach Glen Echo, Gina sheds her stockings; her legs are bare when we arrive. In the parking lot, I take two big handfuls of her skirt and start ripping.

Mrs. Fargo

Mrs. Fargo, your first-grade teacher who committed suicide halfway through the school year, shows up at your Christmas party in a tight red blouse. Your fiancée is not pleased. She knows you have a thing for Mrs. Fargo, a thing dating back to the first day of school when you met Mrs. Fargo's cool patience and heard her cigarette-rough voice pronounce your name.

At seven, you could not add up the parts of her: black nylons like silky cobwebs, so unlike the granny beige your older sister wore; pointy ankles, which you would now describe as "slender"; red hair your mother called an "auburn shag"; the blouse with all the circles on it. You stared deep into those circles during math, some of them formed by crescent moons joined at their tips. The blouse had a scarf, and you remember one of its ends resting on Mrs. Fargo's shoulder like a gentle hand when she turned to write on the board. Now, when you wonder if you've become the kind of man Mrs. Fargo would approve of, you try again to add up her parts, but all you can think of are the red and green crescent moons making circles on the white field of her blouse.

She leans now on the shoulder of a first-grade classmate of yours, and they watch a roulette wheel spin. Your fiancée hisses in your ear: Would you please tell Mrs. Fargo that redheads can't wear red? You pat her arm as if to say, "Now, now," or, "Yes, yes." Either way, it's a dismissive pat.

Mrs. Fargo turns to face you. She smiles so her emerald eyes are happy slits. Sometimes adults get so sad, she says. You nod as if to say, "I know," but what do you know? You believe you could help her because you are grown—not some little boy sitting behind a desk, all round head and big eyes. She swirls her drink in a heavy cut-glass tumbler. It's a whirlpool in her glass, and it reminds you of the time you and your friends swam the perimeter of the pool, creating a current so strong you gave yourselves up to it, tumbling and bumping along the concrete edges.

You tell Mrs. Fargo about winning the fifth-grade spelling bee, and how you kept your ribbon tucked inside the Christmas card she gave you the week before she'd shot herself in the basement of her home. You are saying, "Look at all I have become." Mrs. Fargo takes a sip from her glass, from the swirling froth of it, smiles at you, nods. She surveys the room, full of your first-grade classmates who are now confused adults doing the best they can, which in some cases means making a big mess of it. Baby birds, she says. You're all still baby birds.

One of your former classmates, Douglas Percy, explains a magic trick to Mrs. Fargo.

You see, Mrs. Fargo, he says.

Please, she says, beaming, call me Mars.

Douglas Percy's pink-rimmed eyeballs vibrate in their sockets. In second grade, while ice-skating, he vanished down a dirty slush hole in Turkey Swamp. He continues:

You see, Mars, I have a fake thumb.

He brandishes a plastic thumb, cunningly flesh-colored, which covers his own. From it he draws orange and yellow silk scarves. Then he reaches toward Mrs. Fargo and pulls from behind her ear yards and yards of orange and yellow silk. Mrs. Fargo holds her hand to her chest and says, Oh, Percy! You hope the Vanishing Doomed Boy trick is next, though in his short life you never wished him harm, and were always grateful his tricks worked.

This is no place for boys, you say, but no one listens.

Your fiancée is back. She is hissing again: Do not let another person from your past into this room. You giggle into your drink. I mean it, she says.

But it's Mr. McShane, the librarian who used to visit Mrs. Fargo's classroom and read to you and the class while you sat on the carpet that smelled of Fritos. During lunch, while you blew bubbles in your milk, Mr. McShane and Mrs. Fargo would stand in the open doorway, Mrs. Fargo murmuring, twirling a piece of her hair. You watched, clenching the straw between your puckered lips until they went numb.

Now, as then, Mr. McShane doesn't know you exist. He walks up behind Mrs. Fargo with his fingertips extended, like Nosferatu or Bela Lugosi. He lightly touches the tips of her hair with the tips of his fingers.

Mars, he says.

She closes her eyes; her drink tips forward, piddles onto the carpet.

Mars, he says again.

As you watch the two of them, one of the lunch ladies offers to peel your orange. You let her, and the juice sprays your face and hers.

Don't let the first grade get you down, she says.

It's not the first grade, your fiancée says.

Mrs. Fargo feeds you a segment of orange.

You just keep growing up, she says.

That's what I've been doing, you say. Now that you have her attention, you tell her about your new job, for which you've had to buy suits, and your clear-complexioned fiancée, whose smart cynicism makes you wince. Mrs. Fargo stares at you, a polite, expectant smile on her face. You stare back, becoming and becoming—your tiny offering.

Pedagogy

I

I wanted to impress upon my students the deadly seriousness of their education. They were a soft but kind bunch of loafers, given to grogginess at noon and good-natured self-deprecation. They came to class in slippers and pajama bottoms, and they listened to me with nonjudgmental goodwill. They took notes. They never questioned anything I said. "What do you think?" I'd ask, and they'd shrug, smiling helplessly.

I wanted them to know that what they did here mattered, that the wrong choices or inattention would cost them later. They would wake up in the middle of their lives, not recognizing their surroundings, without a road map or any idea where they might go. I tried to relate this to Rosie at home. She smiled sweetly at my concern, her guitar cradled in her arms, waiting for me to shut up so she could go back to playing it. "They'll be fine," she said. "There's nothing wrong with *them*." But she didn't see their blank faces turned toward her expectantly, waiting for information or insight that would transform them and the world they knew into something meaningful and august.

I tried to tell them, but like many of today's university students, they were not auditory learners. I needed a visual, something to convey with visceral certainty what words could not. So after class one day, in my kitchen—long after Rosie had gone—with the aid of rubber gloves and a pressure cooker, I boiled my head. The meat fell away from the skull, and I scraped the bone clean of cartilage and the sinewy muscles of the jaw. I scraped and bleached my skull until it was so white it looked blue. My new white head rested incongruously atop my tanned neck. Dissatisfied, I sliced from my neck the skin and fat and muscle. Away it went, slapping wetly into the stainless steel sink. Getting the meat from between the vertebrae was a trick. The result was aesthetically pleasing. My new white spine and skull floated above my shirt collar. I was a living example of the seriousness of higher education. "Learning need not be fun," I said to my skull in the mirror. I liked the way I looked; my hollow eye-pits corresponded to my sense of inner calm.

The next morning, for dramatic effect, I arrived two minutes late for class. For a moment, my students were silent. Hillary, with her platinum hair, spoke first. She read the news for the campus TV station, and her anchorperson aspirations gave her a sense of civic-mindedness. In the classroom she modeled good citizenship and wide-eyed attentiveness.

"Is it Halloween?" she asked.

They ascertained it was not. Rick, one of the brighter students, said, "It's Professor. Are you all right?"

"How do you know it's him?" Hillary asked.

"I recognize his tie."

I clacked my jaws at them, but the words wouldn't come; what I'd said in the mirror the night before had been, perhaps, a leftover thought floating in the emptiness like so much ambient noise. I wrote some page numbers on the board, with instructions to discuss them in small groups.

Aside from an occasional surreptitious glance in my direction, the class progressed as many had before. The students conferred in small groups, then presented their thoughts. How could they carry on as though nothing were out of place? At the end of the period, several students made a point of stopping by the front of the room to say good-bye. I elected not to judge my experiment hastily; it would take time, perhaps, for the message to sink in.

II

Over the following days, in my mailbox I found a coupon for a free "stress-management massage," as well as a card from Hillary Evans, the would-be broadcaster, thanking me for all that I do. On my apartment doorstep one day a basket waited for me, filled with packets of cocoa, a tin of hibiscus tea, a box of water crackers, individually wrapped ladyfingers, a smoked summer sausage, and wedges of soft processed cheese. I bumped my head on the door when I bent to retrieve it, and the dry squeak of my skull scraping the wood sent a chill down my spine. Later, in the mirror, I would see that a chalky streak of green paint had transferred itself to my skull. The neighbor boy, who must have heard the thump, opened his door. He held a book I had loaned him, and when he looked up at me he gasped.

"Sir?" He was unfailingly polite. "That you?"

I nodded.

"I finished the book. It was good."

The book was a Hardy Boys mystery, my own copy from boyhood. I had been loaning Henry books since he and his family had moved in next door. I didn't know where they had come from. One morning I opened my door to get the paper, and the landing was filled with their broken, sagging cardboard boxes and piles of toys and bad-smelling clothes. All Henry's siblings had old-style names, too: Victoria and Percy, Rutherford and Hazel. Henry's deep brown hands were thin and dry, the skin on the verge of cracking. I held up a finger and motioned for him to wait. I made him put out his palms, and I squirted cocoa butter onto them. His smile was soft and shy, and he thanked me carefully. I loaned him another Hardy Boys and gave him the cocoa butter.

Inside, I brewed a pot of hibiscus tea and watched its red color deepen while the steam rose and formed beads of condensation where my upper lip would have been. I sat at the counter, hovering over my tea until the cup grew cold. I slept at night, of that I'm sure. When I put my head on the pillow, the ambient noise in my skull was amplified, and it calmed me.

III

Hillary devised a technique for me to communicate with the class. I rapped once on the table for no, twice for yes, and three times for my favorite response: "That's an interesting idea. What do the rest of you think?" which, as Hillary pointed out, is another way of saying "No."

Rick, a physics major, suggested something along the same lines, involving a rigged buzzer or a series of buzzers.

"Like a game show," Hillary said.

"No," I rapped, and I wrote on the board: *Your education is not a game.* I tried to look stern, but what is more stern than a death's-head? On a whim, I wrote, *What's the prize?* They laughed and gave answers I expected: A case of beer! An A for the semester! Exemption from the final! Hillary, the only student who ever bothered to raise her hand, raised her hand. "The prize would be your having dinner with the winner and her—or his—parents." My lower jaw clacked open. "I think he likes that idea," one of the boys said, and the class laughed. Things were certainly more lively; the change in my appearance had shaken them from their complacency. On my way home I purchased a small notebook in which to write about the results of my experiment.

I longed to rush home and tell Rosie, but of course she was long gone. I had come home one day and found her guitar and suitcases by the door. She'd been a student of mine one fall, ten years before we started dating. I had been flush with excitement for the transformative powers of public education. Rosie had won a scholarship in part for her intelligence and in part for having come from a place the admissions committee had never heard of. She maintained eye contact during my first lecture, and after class she came up to the lectern. She didn't have a notebook or a pen with her, as if she'd assumed in advance that nothing I said would be worth taking down.

"Are you for real?" she said.

"Pardon me?" I said.

She shook her head as if to scold and then walked away. For the rest of the semester, she sat at the back, not taking notes but silently judging me. Every day before class, I hoped she would drop. She didn't.

On my end-of-semester evaluation she wrote, "You and the class should spend a semester abroad—in Newark. GET REAL." She signed her name to the form, which I found both thrilling and insulting.

A few years after she dropped out, I began to see her name in the *City Paper*, with listings of her band's performances. The early dates were in family pizza parlors and coffee shops. When the band's picture appeared on the cover of the *City Paper*, I was impressed. She was selling a CD and donating most of the profit to fund an after-school program in her old neighborhood. Her songs, the article said, "artfully touch upon personal responsibility and the bonds of humanity."

Over a post-show tequila, I told Rosie about the service-learning program I had helped launch for the university. She was impressed when I told her about our privileged and sheltered students venturing into the inner city to assist understaffed nonprofits. I didn't tell her that several of the leaders of these organizations had asked me to withdraw my student workers; their work was so erratic and rife with errors and generally shapeless and wobbly, they were more a hindrance than a help. We made plans to meet the following night for dinner. It didn't take long for Rosie to detect that I was a sham.

IV

Rick rigged an electronic device and told lovingly of the details of its fabrication. Three lighted buttons adorned the controls.

"I coordinated them by your tie colors," he said. "You wear the salmon-colored tie a lot. I think it's your favorite, so I made the correct-answer button salmon."

The button was indeed salmon-colored and salmon-shaped. When depressed, it emitted a pleasant mellow tone, something along the lines of middle C on a vibraphone.

"Look," Rick said. "It's like it's jumping. Anyway, I figured positive feeling, positive image, right?

"I've never seen you wear a yellow tie, so I figured you don't like yellow. Plus 'a lemon' is usually a bad thing, so I made the wrong answer button a lemon." He snapped his fingers. "Slick, huh?" This button emitted a minor chord when depressed, the sound of which on a soap opera might introduce a particularly grim segment—the tragic death of a youth or the beginning of the uninterruptible downward spiral of a beloved character.

"Now, for your favorite response—'That's an interesting idea . . . what does the class think?' Mostly you wear blue ties when you're not wearing the salmon, so I figured that's your default choice. So this one's blue wavy lines, like water." This tone had an expectant air, a bright and chirpy quality.

The class was silent a moment. "It's oblique," he admitted. "I wasn't totally happy with it, but I had, like, five papers due this week and I had to make a decision."

I nodded. My lower jaw creaked open. I pushed it shut.

"You like it?" he asked.

I patted his shoulder and nodded more vigorously. I wanted to tell him how proud I was—that this was by far the most thoughtful piece of work he had produced all semester. I was also pleased with his use of the word "oblique." I turned to the board and wrote: *Let the games begin.* The class cheered.

V

First Prize: Dinner with Professor
    An "A" for the semester
    Exemption from final
Second Prize: Exemption from final
Third Prize: A twenty-five-dollar gift certificate to campus bookstore

Third prize was my idea. They nodded graciously and shrugged their assent. We all knew that the real competition would be for first and second prize.

VI

Word of my classroom proceedings got around. My colleagues as-sumed I would write a paper on my experiment, and I was a given a research grant I hadn't applied for. I reimbursed Rick for his materials. Our class sessions were taped so that I might present my technique at conferences for educators. A woman from the Disabilities Resource Center contacted me about giving a talk.

Attendance was at 100 percent. As I meandered around the room with my buzzer (Rick had made it wireless, granting me freedom of movement), I glanced at their books and noted the many highlighted passages and earnestly scribbled marginalia. I remembered an old law-school trick—to highlight the assigned passages as if they had been assiduously read and apprehended when in fact they had not been —and accordingly, I instituted a policy of random checks. Correct answers were awarded a point. Incorrect answers were penalized with a deduction of one point. With funds from my grant, I hired a graduate assistant to keep score in class. The students also competed with daily written assignments in response to my e-mailed questions. It came to my attention that a group of students had begun meeting outside class three times a week to anticipate questions I might ask and to formulate answers. I felt it necessary to institute another policy: if their grades slipped below a C in other classes, they would be disqualified from the competition. They seemed relieved, as if I had saved them from themselves. Their renewed engagement in their learning proved to me that sometimes an act of desperation is exactly what is called for.

VII

At the grocery store, an elderly woman said to her husband that she thought I might be Mexican, or possibly a skinhead. I think she got the idea that I might be Mexican from the Day of the Dead figures on display at the university's museum—the grinning death's-head mariachi strumming their guitars. The skinhead business I could only attribute to deep semantic confusion. Her husband, a grizzled farmer, pursed his lips and took his time answering.

"He hasn't got any skin on his head, Cora. He can't be a skinhead."

She crooked her bony finger at me. "Well, what would you call that?"

"I don't guess they have a name for it yet."

They gazed openly at me. I wanted to explain my position, that I wasn't a skinhead or a Mexican—though there's nothing wrong with being Mexican—that I was in fact a teacher.

"Maybe we should pray for him," she said. "Whether he's a Mexican or a skinhead or what, he looks like he could use some prayer."

"We all could," her husband said.

"Amen," she said.

My jaw dropped—the hinges had become quite loose. The farm wife gasped and pulled the neck of her blouse tight. I turned to the housewares aisle for some wire. A pregnant stock clerk in a green smock helped me select the proper gauge. She unspooled a length and gazed from it to my jaw. She held out her hand as if to touch me, and I took a half-step back, without meaning to. "You mind?" she said. "I need to feel the weight of your jaw." I moved closer and found myself enjoying the cool touch of her fingertips. "This'll do," she said. "Save your receipt, just in case." She regarded me more closely. "It's a good thing you came in. I don't know what's holding you together up there." She walked with me to the checkout line. "You teach at the university. I seen your picture in the paper. I know I'm not supposed to say 'I seen,' and if I was writing a paper I wouldn't."

I nodded at the young woman, holding my jaw shut.

"I read the article about what you're doing. Maybe I might've stayed in school longer if I'd a had you."

I stopped and removed a small notepad I kept in the breast pocket of my jacket. I wrote her an invitation to sit in on my class.

She rested her hand on her belly as she read. "Well, that's nice, but I have to work. Why don't you come sit in on my job while I do it? You can watch me stock shelves." She laughed at her joke and handed me the note.

The young checkout clerk wore gold earrings up and down the rims of both ears. Her rouged cheeks and her fat face had a powdery finish that wasn't altogether unpleasant. In fact, the cosmetically enhanced bloom of her skin appealed to me. I saluted her. She giggled. "You're cute," she said. "Your eyes are so big and round." She giggled again, and beneath her makeup, at the hairline, her color deepened. "I mean, whatever you call them. Your not-eyes are so round."

I took the pad from my pocket and wrote: *I think you mean my "ocular pits."*

She read the note. "Ocular pits. How cool is that?"

I shrugged. She handed me the wire and leaned her hip against the register. "Were you born that way?"

I shook my head.

"Was it an accident?" Again, I signified that that was not the case.

"You did it on purpose!"

I nodded vigorously.

"Oh! Like a tattoo or piercing or gauging—"

I waved my arms frantically as if to erase what she'd said. *Not a fashion statement,* I wrote. *Something more important.*

She nodded. "I totally get it. It's what you're about. It shows the world who you really are, how you want to be seen."

We stared at each other for a moment. I wrote on my pad. *How do I want to be seen?*

"You want to be taken seriously."

I nodded once, sharply, my assent. I invited Dawn the cashier for donuts and coffee before my next morning's class. *My treat,* I wrote. She accepted.

VIII

I had become accustomed to classroom visitors. We had created a gallery of sorts, a line of chairs against the far end of the room where visitors could arrange themselves before class started. And the eternal video camera, which recorded my every move during class—I had forgotten its presence entirely. Outside class, I learned to expect the stares of others, and I turned my gaze inward so as not to notice. I reflected on the success of my project and how helpful it might be to other educators; these thoughts compensated for my lack of privacy in public. But even in my home, I had begun to feel I was never truly alone. Peripheral movement and sudden strange noises startled me from my day-to-day activities. While folding laundry in my bedroom, I felt I played a minor role in a little-watched show: Comedy? Drama? Reality? I could never be sure, though I sensed a disappointing lack of drama.

The only time I felt reasonably comfortable was watching the evening news. It seemed then I could shake the feeling of being under observation —perhaps because I was so engrossed in the programming? Not likely, though it was the only television in which I indulged. In a small and perverse way, I enjoyed the student broadcast. The students gave a sweet imitation of what the grownups did on the networks, mimicking inflections and mannerisms, though at times their speech was so hurried and garbled, with the accented syllables falling so strangely, that I often couldn't understand large portions of the broadcast. I winced at their too-heavy makeup and overstyled hair. I sighed over their cheap suits, which called forth memories of my early days teaching, when I was fresh from graduate school and Men's Wearhouse discount racks. The students reminded me of kittens batting crumpled napkins, in preparation for real hunting. I sometimes became teary-eyed imagining all they might do, when their lives began in earnest.

So I was surprised when, enjoying my few moments of comfortable solitude, I found myself the subject of a three-part investigative feature by reporter and anchor Hillary Evans. My second-grade photo showed in the background over Hillary's shoulder. I leaned closer to the screen. How had she acquired it? My mother appeared. "He was a very serious student, oh yes." Her cotton-candy hair filled the upper two-thirds of the screen. When had she gotten so old? "He was a sensitive child." I groaned. "He was . . . troubled by things."

Next, my high school biology teacher, Mrs. Brown, appeared. She looked much the same as when I knew her; in fact, she seemed not to have changed at all. When she spoke, I detected a faint ring of nostalgia and the hollow tone of disappointment. "I still remember his final project. He was one of my most talented students." Mrs. Brown had hoped I would blossom under her care into a botanist—a better, more successful version of herself.

The manager of the IGA where I'd bagged groceries in high school stood in his red vest in front of the customer service desk. "Oh, yeah. He used to deliver the day-old bread to the food bank. The produce, too. He was a good kid. Never had any trouble with him." He smiled. "We used to tease him. Used to tell him he could work for us if the college thing didn't pan out. I never thought he was a big thinker or nothing. Just sorta quiet." He looked a little uneasy and glanced off-camera. "That's why I'm surprised to hear you say he teaches college. I wouldn't a pegged him as the smartest guy here." Then he shrugged and grinned. "What do I know? I'm just a grocery manager." Laughter ensued off-camera.

Hillary cut in. "Next week we'll hear more about this mysterious young man who was, as his mother said, 'troubled by things.' How did his sensitivity affect his choices as an adult, and how does he influence his students today?"

How *does* he influence his students today? I turned off the television and gathered up the sprawling city of untouched bowls of soup and cups of tea that populated the coffee table. After I deposited them in the sink I stopped by the hall mirror. My suit jacket hung off me. I was surprised to find myself stung by my old boss's comment. I moped around the apartment for the rest of the night. In between moping and pacing, I made cherry Jell-O for Henry and his siblings, whose mother worked the night shift.

IX

I met Dawn at The Donut Hole the next morning. I felt quiet and interior and wished I hadn't made the date. I bought her the elaborate frozen coffee drink she requested and a jelly donut. She pulled the donut apart, eating it tuft by fluffy tuft. She licked the jelly from the center, then tore the rest of it to pieces and ate that, too. She talked about the tattoo parlor her boyfriend was trying to open.

"You should paint stuff on your skull," she said.

I turned my palms up and shrugged elaborately.

"I don't know," she said. "Whatever you're about."

I tilted my head back quickly, and my skull slapped against the vinyl back of the booth.

"Or maybe just something arty and pretty."

I realized the folly of seeking reassurance from Dawn. Rosie, on the other hand, had a way of putting things into perspective. If I told her what my grocery boss had said, she'd shrug and say, "So, you're not the smartest bag boy. There are worse fates." And she'd be right.

After breakfast with Dawn, I came to work to find an envelope underneath my door. I stepped on it as I walked into my office. Inside, I found a note: *The smart kids are selling the dumb kids their questions and answers. Thought you should know.*

It was signed *A Concerned Party.* I couldn't tell who had written it.

I was angry, of course, and then felt foolish. Things had been going too well. Their grades across the board were too high. I had wanted to attribute their success to my superior abilities to teach and motivate. I should have known better. On the other hand, so what if they were getting potential questions and answers from each other? The students who had formulated the questions and answers were thinking and learning, whereas the "dumb" students buying the questions and answers weren't. They would stay dumb; their loss, though I cringed to think what they would do out in the world, what kind of culture they would create with their compromised ethics, their cultivated laziness, their bought-and-paid-for flabby intellects.

In class I had trouble concentrating. I couldn't help trying to deduce which students were involved. The students too looked less enthusiastic, as if all the fun had gone out of the game. I gave my graduate assistant control of the classroom, and for the most part I simply observed. As I watched, I became angrier and angrier. Finally I stopped the class and wrote on the board: *I know you've been cheating. Some of you have been selling your questions and answers.*

I expected embarrassment or outrage. Rick arched an eyebrow and looked around the room. Hillary sat back with her arms folded, watching.

One of the average students said, "How do you know?"

I have my ways, I wrote on the board.

Someone else shrugged.

I wrote, *Why?*

"It's just a game," I heard someone say.

I wrote on the board, *It's your education. Are you going to cheat through life?*

They stared at me as if to say, What did you expect? I understood I was wasting their time. They had careers to start, houses to buy,

families to make. School was for them an anteroom to their final des-
tinations—something to be gotten through with as much attention as
one gives the waiting room at the doctor's office.

I stopped going to class. A week or so later, I peeked in to see the
desks arranged in a circle and students listening as the graduate assistant lectured. Once in a while a student would raise his or her hand.
The video camera and gallery were gone.

Hillary came to my office to visit. "The game got stale after a while.
We got bored with it."

I wrote, *But you were bored before.*

She shrugged. "It's school. Isn't it supposed to be boring?"

She asked if she could interview me for the third installment of her
profile. The second, she said, would air that night. I agreed. Later, she
e-mailed a list of questions, most mundane, except for one: "How has
your illness affected your teaching philosophy?"

I don't have an illness, I typed. After I clicked "send" I settled down
to watch Hillary's broadcast. The picture over her shoulder this time
came from my Web site—a fairly current photo. For this segment, she
had interviewed students and colleagues. The students were kind, and
from my colleagues came an air of strained politeness. Hillary interviewed the custodian who emptied the trash and waxed the floors in
our building. "I don't really know the guy," he said. "He never throws
anything out." This was true; I had 4 five-drawer file cabinets in my
office. "There's just a cup of red tea in his trash every day." He paused
and looked into the camera. "I don't think I'm supposed to tell you
that. What's in his trash. I will say this: he doesn't leave black scuff-
marks on the floor. Man knows how to pick up his feet. More than I
can say for some people." He glanced down, presumably at Hillary's
anchorwoman pumps. I thought it kind of Hillary to end this segment
on a more positive note; I may not have been the smartest bag boy at
the IGA, but I knew how to pick up my feet.

But we weren't finished. On the screen I saw myself at the grocery
store with the green-smocked stock clerk, then at The Donut Hole
with Dawn the cashier. The camera showed Henry and his sister Vic-

toria waving good-bye one morning as I left for school. The camera lingered on their faces and Hillary spoke: "Friends and neighbors alike worry about this dedicated professor. Some say he may be burning the candle at both ends. Tune in next week to find out how his dedication has affected his mental and physical health, and how his illness has affected his teaching." The final shot framed me in my apartment, hovering over my nightly cup of hibiscus tea.

I clutched a pillow to my chest. I wondered if Hillary had video of me with my skull sandwiched between two pillows. I planned to give her plenty of opportunity to catch me in that position. The white noise in my skull soothed me—an absorbing aural narcotic. I flopped over on the couch and listened to the phone ring. Rosie spoke to my machine. "Are you dead? Pick up. I know you've been watching this." She sighed. "Fine. I'll come by."

She sat at my kitchen table with a beer in front of her. She'd made me change out of my suit and she inspected my body. "You're turning into a skeleton. You have to eat."

I gestured helplessly to my mouth.

"We'll get you an IV or a stomach tube."

I waved my hand at her.

"Why did you do this to yourself?"

My heart glowed in my chest; of course, she alone would intuit that I'd had some intention—that I'd tried to do something. I explained, in writing, what I'd attempted.

"It didn't work, did it?" She seemed smaller, without her usual energy and bravado.

I wrote, *How are the after-school programs?*

She took a long drink from her beer before answering. "Fine. A ten-year-old shot his seven-year-old cousin. A guidance counselor tried to date a middle-school student. We can't get the parents to stop beating on their kids, and we can't get the kids to stop touching each other. They're having oral sex, you know. The kids. In middle school."

I started at this and pounded my fist on the table. I took up my pen and began to write, but she stopped me. "Don't change the subject.

Why didn't you call me before you did this? I could have told you it wouldn't work."

I had to try, I wrote.

The doorbell rang. It was Henry, with the empty dessert cups. He had washed them, and their cut-glass facets reflected the grays and browns of the hallway.

He handed me a small bundle. "My mama made this for you." In the light of the foyer, I unrolled it. It was a knit hat, made of thick, soft yarn. The colors ran from deep russet at the crown to paler shades of melon and tangerine. "I have one, too, but mine is green. We all have one."

I put the hat on and wished I could have smiled. I nodded and patted Henry's shoulder and gave him a thumbs-up. After he left, I modeled the hat for Rosie. "The colors are a nice distraction," she said. I put my thumbs where my ears would have been and waggled my fingers at her. In the kitchen, I cut up the summer sausage and arranged the slices on a plate with the cheese and crackers.

"I've been meaning to write you," she said. "Or call."

Why? I wrote.

"To see how you're doing?"

How I'm doing, I wrote. *I'm quitting my job.*

She didn't seem surprised. "I thought you loved it."

I shook my head. *I loved what I thought I could do.*

The doorbell rang again. The custodian who had talked about my trash on television stood in the doorway, still dressed in his tan uniform. He apologized for revealing the contents of my wastebasket. I was touched by his shame over what he perceived to be an ethical breach. I waved away his apology, gestured him in, and gave him a beer. He inspected my floors with professional interest. I was glad to have recently cleaned but nervous about the quality of my housekeeping.

The three of us sat around the table. He didn't look at me as he spoke. I realized he had never seen me in anything but a suit, and I felt underdressed. Rosie refused to call him by the name embroidered on his shirt. She said, "Mr.— . . . ," drawing out the *r,* until he supplied his surname. Mr. Morgan lived outside town, where rents were cheaper.

His grandfather had been a custodian at the university, and so had his father. He and Rosie talked about the unionization of the custodial staff, which Mr. Morgan thought necessary and unfortunate. I listened to them talk about health care and the living wage. As dusk fell, I longed for their conversation to end. I needed to listen to the static in my head.

A Message from the Water

Think of them now, the drowned boys, as you float on your back in the flat dark of the nighttime Gulf. The water laps against your ears. Your girlfriend splashes nearby, occasionally brushing by you, her slippery skin an invitation. Think of them now: the foaming water of the New York swimming hole, the boys standing round it. Nothing here moves that fast. You've heard stories about locals who've gone into underwater tunnels to investigate slow-moving rivers flowing underground. They put on their gear—oxygen tanks, lamps, fins—and disappear into a gently swirling current. They try to follow the river to the place where it emerges, but it's darker than they imagined; there are twists and turns. You could tell them, "You won't come out," but they go, with warnings, encouragement, or indifference.

You stand and pinch the water from your nose. Your girlfriend floats on her stomach, in imitation of the dead. Her brown hair spreads around her. You take a breath and dive under her, swimming low, scraping the mucky bottom with your hands. When you surface, she is still floating. You take a bigger breath and shoot out, deeper into the Gulf. The water feels cooler. You swim and swim, hearing only vague liquid sounds and the occasional crack of your joints. When you spring out of the water, you gasp for air. She calls your name. You don't answer. You like the sound of her voice. You like that she sounds afraid.

"Over here," you say, waving your arms. She swims toward you.

You float on your back again. Did each one think he would be the one to save the others? Did they know they were drowning? They would have tried to swim, flailing through the mist of whitewater, punching through the churning hydraulic, scraping at the sharp rocks at the bottom of the hole. You imagine them curled under the surface of all that turbulence.

The girl reaches you, touches your arm. You stare into her eyes, at the wet triangles of lashes. Her breath comes in short gasps. You take her hands, treading water with just your legs.

She giggles. "I'm tired."

"There's nothing to hurt you," you say.

She tilts her head back, re-wets her hair. "That which doesn't kill us makes us stronger."

"The unexamined life isn't worth living."

She spits water at you, struggling to get away. "Only the good die young."

You grip her wrists tighter. "Elementary, my dear Watson."

She laughs, struggles. "Now I'm really tired." She tries to pull away but you hold on. Her chin dips below the water. A cross look passes over her face.

"Are you really tired, or do you just think you are?"

She kicks you in the gut—not hard—and you release her. She swims away quickly. Your gut muscles feel fatigued. You imagine taking her out for breakfast in the morning—pancakes with syrup and butter—then napping soundly in the truck before driving home to sleep in your bed. You'll wake in time for dinner, when your parents will ask about your plans for the night—where you will go and with whom. Your father has already once cleared his throat and broached the subject of "being careful" with the girl. You nodded and cut him off. You assumed he was talking about sex, and he probably was, but why say it that way? Why say, "Be careful with that girl"? Why not say, Be careful not to get her pregnant. Be careful not to waste your time. Be careful not to bore her or yourself. Be careful of being too careful.

You swim back to shore, drag yourself from the water. Your legs feel light and heavy at the same time. Your girlfriend stands naked at the shoreline, her arms outstretched.

"What're you doing?" you ask.

"Standing here," she says.

You lie on the sand. You hear the roar of whitewater in the swimming hole in New York. You see the boys dive in, one after another. Maybe they hit their heads on rocks, were knocked unconscious, made unaware of their fate. Maybe they plunged in and were turned over and over. Maybe they hoped the roiling would stop. They should have known—shouldn't they?—that they'd never come out. Anyway, they wouldn't be able to hear anything over the roar, if any one of them had been able to shout a message from the water. Maybe they watched one another jump in and disappear until there was only one left. He would have jumped in knowing that the others were drowning, that he would too.

The girl fills your belly button with sand. She sprinkles a line from your navel up your chest, to the hollow at the base of your throat. You wish she needed you for something, or that someone did. You search her eyes. A piece of shell sticks to her cheek. You scrape it away with your fingernail. Sitting up, you brush the sand from your chest. She huddles between your legs, and you wrap your arms around her, both of you watching the water. Small waves lick at the dirty shore. You feel a churning and tumbling inside you, and the roar of it sounds in your ears. You put your lips on the girl's hair, close your eyes, and murmur, "We must."

Cake

I was on hold at work. Slumped in my chair, with the phone trapped between my shoulder and my head, I stared past the computer screen out the window. I was hoping for snow—lots of it—enough to cover the sleeping, wet landscape of Maryland. Three days before Thanksgiving, and someone had hung an accordion-crepe-paper turkey from the drop ceiling. It swayed above us. I looked it right in the eye and sang along with the Muzaked Sonny & Cher.

My other line rang. Karen picked it up, even though I'm supposed to answer her lines, and Gloria's, too. I could see her from my desk, and I could tell it was Ren calling. He made stupid jokes to Karen whenever he called me or came to visit, and Karen always laughed. She laughed now, pressed hold, and dangled the receiver over her shoulder. She wheeled her chair around to face me.

"Clarence again," she said. "For you."

I let him wait. A receptionist at St. Peter Medical had me on hold; we were trying to work out a deceased client's bill—Mr. Boyle. We were getting so close to figuring it out, I didn't want to hang up. His wife had sent me a mass card, which I'd tacked up on my partition wall. You'd think once they were gone it would all be over, but the bills still come. I probably got more attached to our clients than an insurance rep should. And I wasn't even a rep—I was a rep's assistant. Ren used to criticize me for that—getting too involved—though at first he'd found it appealing.

My second line went dark, then rang again. I swerved around to look at Karen. She had already picked up. Her shoulders shook with laughter. I threw a Post-it pad at her, hitting her in the shoulder. She turned to look at me. I shook my head. She put Ren on hold again. I finished with St. Pete's and picked up Ren.

"You know what happened?" Clarence never said hello.

"Tell me what happened," I said.

"You got cold." He had been trying to pinpoint the exact reason for our breakup, and whenever an insight flashed he'd call me. I guess he didn't want me to be left in the dark.

"I got cold," I said.

"You got cold, and I felt rejected, so I got cold," he explained.

"I got cold, you felt rejected, so you got cold," I said.

"Yes."

"Over is over. I can't talk to you here."

"Let me take you to dinner."

"Why don't you take Karen to dinner?"

I hung up.

As if I could concentrate, I returned to the letter on my screen, addressed to Mrs. Boyle, wife of the deceased Mr. Boyle. The company had sent a flower arrangement to his funeral, and Mrs. Boyle had sent us a thank-you card, along with her daughter-in-law's recipe for salmon artichoke heart canapés. I don't know why she'd sent it, but I felt it begged acknowledgment.

> Dear Mrs. Boyle:
>
> Thank you so much for the recipe. I'm sure I'll have an opportunity to try it over the holidays. I'll let you know how it turns out.
>
> If you have any questions about your new policy, or if you decide to make changes, don't hesitate to call me. Have a safe and happy holiday.
>
> Yours,
> Penny Straithorn

My line rang, and I snatched it up. "Clarence," I said. "What?"

"You're jealous." He sounded happy.

"I'm jealous? You're sick," I said and hung up.

It was four o'clock, a little too early to leave. I shut my computer down, put on my sweater, and shoved in my chair. I tapped Karen on the shoulder.

"I'm outta here."

She swiveled toward me. "There's a chili contest at the bar tonight. You should come."

Karen's main hobby was hanging out at Rumors downtown. I went once. It was the kind of bar where young brides-to-be had their bachelorette parties and all the girls who weren't getting married tried to unveil the soon-to-be bride. I had no desire to watch spandex-clad undergraduates yank veils and eat chili.

"No thanks," I said. "You have fun."

In the Chevette, I pulled out my list. It was cold, too cold to drive right away, so I let the heater run while I squirmed in my seat and perused my list of Things to Do Before Holiday. "Cake" was something I could tackle tonight. I had a mix in the pantry but no pans, for reasons having to do with Clarence's goldfish. No problem—I would pass an Ames on my way home.

The parking lot smelled of wet cardboard, and every pothole was filled with exhaust-and-oil-sullied snow. A large black woman with jingle-bell earrings pushed her toddler in a cart so jangly it made *my* teeth feel as though they might shake loose. The kid was vocalizing, letting all the bumps jar his voice in and out of pitch. I smiled at him. The mother said something that sounded threatening, and he fell silent. I tried to play peek-a-boo with him, from a distance, behind his mother's back, but he was having none of that. He looked at me, then up at her, then at me again. No more fun and games, his eyes seemed to say. Now's a bad time.

The store was decorated for Christmas already. I'd been in denial about the holidays, though usually I enjoy them very much. Ren and I had broken up a month ago; I had just left his goldfish, Jaster, in a cake pan on the stoop of his brother's house. Before we'd broken up, we'd had plans to go to his parents' house for Thanksgiving. After a month of not talking, since I'd returned Jaster, Clarence called every day. But no mention had been made of Thanksgiving, or of the holidays to follow. I was putting off making a decision about what to do, mostly because I didn't have any options—no obvious ones, anyway.

So, even though I was enjoying the red and green metallic tinsel strung across the aisles, and the buckets of giant peppermint sticks flanking each checkout lane, I also felt uneasy. Racks of prepackaged bubble bath and bath oils caught my eye; I stopped to poke my finger through the cellophane. Why had I come? Cake pans. I found a set of Teflon-coated heart-shaped pans, with a picture of a finished cake all decorated with swirls of pink frosting.

The stairwell of my apartment building smelled like boiled cabbage. I think it was carpet mold, actually, because no one on my floor seemed the type to boil cabbage, but the smell could have been coming from another floor. My right-hand neighbors' new baby was shrieking, and my left-hand neighbor was screaming awful things about it. He was a pretty nice guy—he always said hi, and he invited me in to look at the improvements he was making in the apartment—but he had problems with anger. I heard him come home from work late some evenings. He'd let the door slam behind him, then clump over to the answering machine and hit play. I could hear the beep, the walls were so thin, and the muffled message. Before it had even played through he would start screaming. I wondered what was wrong with his life to make him so angry.

I stood on the landing in front of my door, between their two doors, wondering what to do. If I knocked on the Screamer's door he would be embarrassed, probably. If I knocked on the Nice Couple's door, they might think I was complaining. Besides, they had their hands full. I decided to do nothing. It would blow over. The shrieking would eventually stop. And I would bake my cake.

I was plumbing the depths of one steaming heart-shaped layer of devil's food cake with a toothpick when the phone rang.

"Yel-lo," I said.

"God, you sound like such a redneck," Ren said.

"Clarence," I said, "how goes it?"

"What're you doing?" he asked.

"Baking a cake," I said, wishing instantly I'd said something more clever, less honest.

He laughed. "You love your sweets, don't you?"

The Eskimos have 248 words for snow; Ren had about that many ways of saying "You're fat."

I sighed. We were way past the crying-into-the-phone stage. Well, I had cried and pleaded and called him in the middle of the night when I knew he wasn't alone. Actually, I hadn't known he wasn't alone until I called. I could tell by the way he talked to me because I'd heard it from the other end before. After a while I gave up. Ren had started calling me again just when I'd stopped crying every day and lifted my head up and started to sniff around.

We talked like we always had—about the people we knew in common, the students he taught at the community college, books we wanted to read, and so on. That the two of us could still chat this way made no sense to me. I guess I didn't have anyone but Clarence to talk to. I found myself laughing; my spirits soared about 100 percent. I let my guard down. Clarence sensed this, and he started in. I sat at the dining-room table with the layers of cooling cake in front of me. I fiddled with the box of toothpicks. Ren's voice grew quiet and intense—the fuck-me-baby voice or the I'm-going-to-whale-on-your-ass voice—they were the same, in my case anyway. The voice had to be placed in context for it to be readable. The situation determines ass-kicking or loving—though it's not always as obvious as it would seem. I know what you're thinking: Anyone with a brain wouldn't confuse hitting and loving. I'm just saying it isn't always crystal clear.

As he worked me over on the phone, talking to me in that low, intense murmur, deep inside, below my gut, there was a glowing red ember, like glass that's been heated until it becomes molten. When Clarence starts in on me, that's all I can feel. When he comes to me his face looks raw, hurt, and vulnerable. He puts his arms around me and hugs so tight and so hard I feel I might disappear. I want to.

Plus, there was the aforementioned case of conversation.

"We had it so good," Clarence said. "What happened?"

I rolled my eyes. I was tired of saying, You broke up with me, remember?

"Did Jaster thaw out?" I asked, instead.

Apparently a thin crust of ice had formed over the cake pan, over Jaster. He wasn't moving much when Ren returned home, late, from who knows where. Not flipping his little goldfish fantail in a jaunty greeting as he usually did. Ren accused me of being spiteful. I insisted that I thought he would be lonely without Jaster, and that Jaster certainly missed him.

"Not that you care," Ren said. "If you did you wouldn't have left him out in the cold."

"You know how they kill diseased fish?" I asked. A guy at the pet shop by the Ames had told me one day when I was buying food for Jaster.

Ren grunted. That meant no.

"Put them in a pan of water in the freezer. Their metabolism slows so it's like they're in a coma? Then you take them out and chop off their heads. With a sharp knife. It's painless. They can't feel a thing. Then you flush 'em. Or whatever."

"Jaster's fine," Ren said. "Why are you baking a cake?"

"Because I feel like it." I poked a toothpick into the side of one layer.

"Are you making it for someone?" Totally transparent.

"It's for me. I like cake," I said.

Ren laughed a little. "You made yourself a cake? Figures. Don't get fat, now."

I slid the pale toothpicks into the sides of the cake, all along the edges, while I sat there trying to get up enough gumption to hang up on him. I wondered what Ren wanted, but I kind of knew. I wasn't going to let him off the hook, though. If he was trying to start something up again, it was going to have to be all him. I wasn't going to be a party to this anymore, not unless he did some serious convincing, of which I was certain he was incapable. I decided then to have a holiday party.

"Look," I said. "I'm really tired. I have to go."

"My folks want to know about Thanksgiving. What should I tell them?"

"Tell them we're broken up," I said, completely neutral, while my heart hammered and I sweated out the pits of my sweater. "I mean, you haven't told them we're broken up?"

"I guess not."

I resisted the urge to slam the phone on the table. I'd already broken three, one for each year of our fabulous courtship.

"What do you think they've been thinking, Clarence? I mean, don't you think they've wondered where I've been these past two months?" We used to see them regularly, for Sunday dinner.

He was rattling pots or something while he was talking to me, and he sounded suddenly distracted. "Uh . . . what?"

"Do you think they might think you've finally killed me?"

He laughed.

"Stuffed me in a barrel and tossed me in the Potomac?"

"Maybe."

"What are you waiting for?"

"I don't know," he said. "I thought you'd come around."

"Come around to what?"

"So I guess I'll just have to broach the subject, because you won't. Let's spend Thanksgiving with my family."

I thought about his mother's multicourse meal—a combination of Italian and standard American: antipasto, ravioli, broccoli rabe, candied yams and carrots, turkey, stuffing, mashed potatoes. Pie later— pecan—and coffee.

"I have plans," I said.

"You do?" he asked.

"Is that so impossible?"

"It's just I know you don't have family—"

I had to get rid of him quickly. "Thanks for the offer, but I'm all set. Tell your folks hi." And I hung up.

My instinct then was to curl up on the couch in front of the TV. Tonight, though, I had a cake to frost. I even colored the frosting pink like the cake in the picture. I stood at the dining-room table looking at it for a while before I went to bed.

I woke to a winter brightness that could only mean sun reflecting off snow. About three inches covered the ground, enough so that no grass poked through. I had plans to take the cake to work. I needed to make some friends. I promised myself I'd go shopping after work. I'd let myself use the credit card. I rarely did that. I never carried a balance; it was strictly for emergencies. I tried not to get too down about the chinos and rose-colored pullover and dirty bucks I wore. I wrapped the cake and made my way to the car, on time for a change. At some time during the night, Ren must have realized it was going to snow—maybe he'd heard the late weather report; sometimes he stayed up well into the morning grading papers. He'd driven over here—thirty minutes from his brother's house—and laid newspaper across my windshield so I wouldn't have to scrape the snow off. It was a little creepy, but he knew better than to leave flowers or a note. That kind of stuff makes me nervous. I rolled the newspaper and snow off the windshield and threw the mess of it in the dumpster.

I worked for two claims adjusters at Atlantic Health, Life, and Indemnity, a huge operation of which we were a very small part dealing with life insurance claims for senior citizens. The company took up the whole of an eleven-story building and only served the Mid-Atlantic region. Other departments dealt with mishaps, misfortune, and tragedies: the entire second floor was devoted to claims related to mental illness; floors five and six handled coronary bypass, angioplasty, heart attacks, strokes, and embolisms; the seventh floor housed personnel trained to evaluate occupational therapy claims.

Karen was about thirty, six years older than I was, and Gloria was in her fifties. I opened their mail and tried to find the files that matched the customer letters. It sounds simple, but the files could be anywhere in the building—on our floor, on a desk in another department (because often people had more than one thing wrong; for instance, Amelia Petty had correspondence in Respiratory Ailments and Theft, her three inhalers and her Pulmo machine having been stolen from her car), or in the file library in the basement. I spent a lot of time looking sideways at shelves or staring down into big file bins. The job had been temporary—I was assigned through an agency while Gloria and Karen interviewed people for the permanent position. I did such a good job keeping up with the correspondence that they decided it would be easier to keep me than to sort through more résumés and schedule more interviews. I decided to stay. It was pleasant enough and seemed better than my other options.

I also typed responses to the letters and sent sympathy cards and fruit baskets or flowers when necessary. At the change of seasons, we sent out one-page newsletters with information about the hazards of that particular time: flu, poison ivy, tick bites, chigger bites, gutter cleaning, fireworks, etcetera. I wrote these. The idea behind the newsletters, of course, was to keep our clients alive as long as possible so the company didn't have to pay out. The holiday newsletter was mainly about getting help for depression and avoiding household fires due to open flames and faulty wiring in Christmas lights. Falling asleep drunk with lighted cigarettes is also a problem during the holidays, but Gloria asked me to leave that out. She was looking at Karen while she said this, and whispering to me. We were well aware of Karen's activities at the bar, as she reported them regularly. Aside from this, I'd only heard Karen speak of holiday meals with her Scottish family. They eat haggis. It's a delicacy, apparently, involving sheep stomachs stuffed with all the parts you wouldn't normally eat, ground up and mixed with spices. Mostly I avoided talking to Karen because I didn't want to end up like her.

Holding the cake platter in front of me, I peeked into Gloria's cubicle. Gloria was at her desk, in her slippers, knitting. She looked up.

"You're here early," she said.

"Yup," I said. "I'm turning over a new leaf."

She shrugged. "OK," she said. She went back to her knitting.

"I brought a cake for us—for break," I said. Normally I didn't participate in breaks, just skirted the periphery of Karen and Gloria's chat. Come to think of it, mostly Karen talked and Gloria worked her needles.

"Honey, I'm on a diet," she said. "What kind of cake?" We planned to meet at 10:20 in the break room.

I had a pile of correspondence waiting in my cubicle. Some early cards from doctors—from their receptionists, more likely—and the usual inquiries and applications and thank-you notes.

> To Whom It May Concern:
>
> Please send information about coverage for people with pre-existing conditions.
>
> Sincerely,
> Mrs. William Sumner

I imagined a giant black lady sitting at the dining room table in her rowhouse. Diabetes, probably, maybe glaucoma. I had acquired a weird instinct about the people who wrote me.

> Dear Mrs. Sumner:
>
> On behalf of Atlantic Health, Life, and Indemnity, it would delight me to send you information about coverage for persons with pre-existing conditions. However, I need to know what the pre-existing conditions are. Please do one of the following, so that we can serve you as quickly as possible:
>
> 1) Contact your doctor's office and have them send copies of your files and the files of all persons to be covered on the policy.
>
> 2) Contact me at the address or phone number below, with your doctor's number so that I can contact him/her for your files.
>
> As a side note, rates will increase after the first of the year. If we act quickly, we can still get you in under this year's rates.
>
> Happy Holidays,
> Penny Straithorn

I use an Oneida stainless-steel letter opener with my initials, in script, to open the letters. It only cost me ten dollars and is much nicer to hold than the plastic letter openers we get from drug companies. Gloria complimented me on it one day.

To the Person Who Writes the Newsletter:

I read what you wrote about "Holiday Blues" and I think I might have that. I called the number for the Clearinghouse for Information on Depression and they gave me a number to call for "group counseling." I don't know about that. Can you give me some information? Anything would be helpful.

Gratefully,
Mrs. Jonathan Peaks

Another Mrs.-Husband's-First-Name-Husband's-Last-Name. The first one I let alone because I could tell from the writing that she was older. It's gotten to the point where I can tell from the writing how old, how sick, how poor, how rich, how sad. Maybe it's a combination of the ink, the paper, the handwriting, the words, the sound. Sometimes I can hear their voices when I read the letters. Anyway, this second one I could tell wasn't old enough to be calling herself Mrs.-Husband's-First-Name-Husband's-Last-Name. Not that it was my business.

Dear Ms. Peaks:

Group counseling can be daunting for some, especially those who are shy, but think of it as making a whole new set of friends who have problems like yours. You'll meet people who will understand how you feel and be sympathetic. Some people will be worse off than you and will remind you that you don't have it so bad. I recommend it; what have you got to lose?

Good luck, and let me know how it goes.

Sincerely,
Penny Straithorn

Karen was out for the day. She had been at Rumors the night before. Gloria told me this while we ate cake midmorning in the break room. Although she didn't comment on the quality of the cake, or tell me how nice I was for bringing it, as I had hoped, the sugar and fat seemed to loosen her tongue, and we talked for a while. She told me how worried she was about Karen. She told me how Karen had cried last week when one of our clients finally died of stomach cancer.

"There's so much death," she said, shaking her head. "You'd think Karen would be more careful."

"What do you mean?" I asked, but I knew what she meant.

"Thanks for the cake, sweetie," she said, shoving away from the table. "Back to the grind."

I invited the guys from Property in. They made much of the cake. I sliced it up and they ate quickly, off napkins, while standing around nodding and grunting in their suits and ties. Alan, the guy in charge of Theft, said, "Anytime you want to bring a cake for us, you just go ahead. Anytime."

"OK," I said. He was cute. Skinny, dark hair, mustache. I liked the way he gobbled his cake and licked the frosting from his fingers. He patted his stomach, crumpled his napkin and threw it in the trash. On the way back to his desk he sang to himself, something that sounded Christmasy.

That afternoon I felt a little nostalgic for Clarence. Once, during better times, he had stopped by the office to have lunch with me. He joked around with Karen, which I didn't like, but then he pulled up a chair next to me, reading over my shoulder as I typed answers to the sick and the sad. It annoyed me at first.

"God, Penny, you really love these people up. I mean, not in a fake way."

I turned to look at him, smiling a little, puzzled.

"It sounds like you really care, is what I mean."

His voice had a metallic ring, and I should have guessed from its flat notes something of the trouble to come. "Well, I do care," I said.

"I don't think just anyone would write letters like this." His voice softened, and I suppose he was wondering about all the nice things I'd do for him. "You're like Dear Abby, Mother Teresa, and a guardian angel rolled into one."

I had laughed, but I'd been touched. I'd never thought of myself that way. He must have thought if I was that caring with complete strangers he was in for something really special. I could only disappoint, of course. Now I sat at my desk, dazed, and mourning those warm feelings. I knew they'd been worn away by Clarence's need. For the rest of the afternoon I sat at my desk and stared from the pile of letters to the computer screen and back again.

It snowed more, and Karen called to say she'd be out tomorrow, too—Could someone drop her files off on the way home? I offered because Gloria looked tired. We walked out together.

"Those pigs in Property ate that whole beautiful cake," Gloria said.

"I don't mind," I said. "I can't eat it all myself. That's the thing about living alone."

"You got a boyfriend or something, don't you?"

"Not anymore," I said. "Not since October."

Gloria was starting to huff and puff. "Well, you're young."

"Yes," I said. "I suppose."

Karen answered the door in a chenille robe. She didn't seem surprised to see me.

"Just put it in here," she said, gesturing to the living room.

The TV was on, with the sound down low. An afghan on the sofa looked as if it had been pushed aside. I set the file box down and glanced at the dining-room table. One end of the table was spread with wax paper, and on it were tiny colored shapes—spheres of varying sizes, little top hats, triangular orange things.

"Marzipan?" I asked.

Karen nodded and smiled. "For my nieces and nephews. I make marzipan snowmen every year for their stockings."

"Neat," I said. I'd never eaten marzipan. I wasn't sure you were supposed to. It seemed more for decoration than anything else. "Well," I said. "Hope you feel better."

She let me out. It was getting colder, and the sky looked like old mashed potatoes gone bad. I was starting to slip into my evening coma when I remembered about shopping. That perked me up a little bit. Enough to get me to the mall.

I successfully charged $423. I had a $750 limit. I replaced my wardrobe of baggy chinos and knit pullovers with cute little skirts and sweaters and tights. At first I found myself drawn to the sale racks, where it's impossible to find anything that goes with anything you already own or anything else in the store. It turns out to be a waste of money because you buy an item that can't be integrated into your wardrobe. I had a closet full of these things—GAP, Limited, Banana Republic—all sale racks are a scam. It's the ugly, ill-fitting crap that no one wanted the first time around. At home, I put most of my old clothes in shopping bags, except for one pair of chinos and one pair of jeans. Then I drove to the Christmas Clothing drop at the Ames parking lot right away, so I wouldn't lose my nerve.

On the day before Thanksgiving, Gloria brought in a fruitcake. We sat at the table in the break room, which was actually a small kitchen at the center of our floor. Gloria was knitting, something small and green. It looked like a cape for a mini-crusader.

"For my dog groomer's new baby," she said. Gloria didn't have any children. She and her husband hadn't wanted any. So they had dogs. I thought it was a lot of trouble to go to for someone who wasn't related to you.

"Do you knit?" she asked.

"No," I said. I remembered in Brownies, sitting in a circle with the other girls who confidently knitted scarves and hats and eventually mittens for their families. My needles kept slipping out of my hands and out of the yarn entirely, clattering on the floor, breaking that industrious girlhood silence. "They couldn't teach me. I was unteachable."

Gloria made a face. "You want to learn? I'll teach you."

I felt I should say yes, though I honestly didn't believe I could be taught.

"I don't know anyone with kids. I mean, who would I make things for?"

"I don't know," Gloria said. "Whoever you want. You got friends, neighbors? Family? It doesn't have to be baby stuff. Make something for yourself."

"Sweaters?"

"Maybe start with something simpler."

"A scarf?"

"Yeah, sure, a scarf. I'll pick out some yarn tonight. Something simple. We'll start tomorrow."

Somewhere I remembered hearing a story about teenaged girls knitting scarves and hats and gloves for GIs during World War II. It seemed you should have someone to knit for. Maybe I could make a present for my college roommate, though we hadn't spoken in a year. Or the New Baby next door. Or maybe I would give my first effort to Gloria. Or Ren's parents. Maybe I would just keep it for myself.

I cleared my throat. "Tomorrow's Thanksgiving," I said.

"Friday, then. We'll do it Friday. You're coming in, right?"

I nodded. Gloria didn't ask what I would be doing for the holiday. I returned to my stack of letters.

> Dear Penny:
>
> Thank you for your kind attention. You've been so very helpful. Since my husband's death I have been trying to stay functional. I get dressed in the morning, I eat breakfast. Just when your letter came, along with the beautiful tulips, I was beginning to think, Why bother? What for? I haven't yet called one of those groups listed on the sheet you sent, but I am thinking about joining the walking group. When the tulips die out, I'm going to plant the bulbs in the yard.
>
> Thank you again for your kindness.
>
> Yours,
> Eleonore Blick

"Well, don't you look nice today." It was Alan, from Theft. "Got any cake for me?"

I looked up from Eleonore Blick's letter. "No cake today. But I'm thinking about having a holiday party. For which I'd make cake. And cookies."

He reached into his jacket pocket and whipped out his Palm Pilot. He flourished the plastic wand and made anxious clucking noises with his tongue. "When?"

"Uh . . . I don't know."

"Girl, you better decide soon. The weekends are filling up."

I was beginning to feel pressured. I guessed there was no backing out now.

"Well," I said. "When are you free?"

We set a date: the second Sunday after Thanksgiving.

"And will you be sending invitations?" His brown eyes looked serious.

"Of course," I said.

"Wonderful." He patted the partition of my cubicle and turned, walking back in the direction of Theft/Property. I stood up to watch him. He had a large head with lots of dark shiny hair, which I found appealing, though I couldn't say why.

At least now I had something to do on Thanksgiving: plan for the party.

After work I drove down the wet streets from Rockville to Wheaton. The traffic lights made patterns like molten glass on the wet asphalt. I went to Phantasmagoria, a record store in the basement of a strip mall. I would need music for my party; plus I could cross something else off my list. Phantasmagoria sold only records— mostly used—and no CDs. I had a turntable and the cassette deck in the car, and that was it. I bought: Marvin Gaye; Bix Beiderbecke; A Cool Yule—Various Artists Play Jazz Renditions of Christmas Favorites; Bing Crosby, White Christmas; The Ellington Units. That would do. The man who checked me out wore a Santa hat. He nodded at my purchases.

"Good choices," he said. He stuffed a flyer in my bag.

"What's that?" I asked.

"Thanksgiving Dance," he said.

"Tomorrow? Here?"

"Yup."

"I like to dance," I said.

"You're in luck, then."

So much went on that I didn't know about. I stuck the flyer to the refrigerator when I got home. On it, a turkey danced below a disco ball.

Before I went to bed, I made a list of people to invite to the party:

1. Left-hand and right-hand neighbors—the Screamer; the Nice Couple with the New Baby
2. Gloria and Husband
3. Karen
4. Alan from Theft/Property
5. Other guys from Theft/Property
6. Anne.

Anne, my college roommate, lived six hours away in Connecticut, but I felt I should invite her anyway.

The phone rang while I was making my list. I figured it was Ren. He had called last night while I was shopping, but I hadn't bothered to call back.

"What?" I said.

"Penny? It's Gloria here."

I apologized. "I thought you were someone else."

"I guess so. Anyways, if you're not doing anything, why don't you come by for dessert tomorrow? That way we can get you knitting right away."

I stretched my legs and wiggled my toes. "Okay," I said. We agreed on six o'clock.

"Only you have to leave by nine, 'cause that's our bedtime," she cackled in that unapologetic older-person way.

My calendar was filling up. Ren didn't call that night, and that was fine with me.

On Thanksgiving morning I listened to my new records while I made invitations on heavy card stock I'd taken from one of my temp jobs. They had it made into scratch pads, but it was really too nice for just doodles and phone messages.

Ren called midmorning.

"'Lo," I said, shouting over the music.

"What time should I come get you?" he said.

"What time should you come get me? I'm not going to be here. I've got plans, I told you."

"You've got plans," Ren said. "Well, I wish you'd told me—"

"I think I did," I said. Had I made some commitment, promised something I couldn't remember?

"You sort of did. I guess I didn't believe you."

I tapped my finger on the tabletop. "You didn't believe me?"

"So, where are you going?"

"Coworker's house," I said.

"Sounds like big fun. Well, bye." He hung up. My heart was knocking against my rib cage, and I suddenly felt very bad about everything. I paced around the living room and dining room and kitchen several times. I stopped in front of the flyer on the fridge. I looked at the memo pad where I had written down Gloria and Howard's address. I went into the bedroom and admired the new satin skirt and fuzzy sweater I'd picked out to wear, with the new pointy black boots. Then I made myself sit down and finish the invitations, though a couple of times I got shaky and had to get up to pace again.

Gloria and Howard lived in a rambler in Rockville. They had two big dogs, both Irish setters who looked to be well fed as well as accomplished countertop food stealers. I bent down to say hi, and one of them licked my lips. He smelled like turkey. "Yuck," I said. Gloria cackled and patted the dog's head.

We had pumpkin pie in the kitchen, with coffee. It was okay pie— not great—but I didn't care. Gloria sprayed whipped cream from a can onto it. I had two pieces. After we finished, Howard excused himself to the den to watch football. Gloria pulled out some multicolored yarn in mottled fall colors—rust, olive, gold. She had written instructions for me on how to start, and she showed me once, then made me take it out and do it myself over and over until I didn't need her to show me. We sat in the quiet kitchen with both dogs under the table. One of them—the one that had licked me—had draped his fat head across my feet, and I could see he was getting my boots wet, but I didn't move. By the time nine o'clock rolled around I had several inches of scarf.

"Keep going," Gloria said at the door. "I want to see some progress tomorrow."

"I won't get much done tonight," I said. "I'm going to a dance."

Gloria made an exclamation of some kind, as if to say she remembered dances. "Have fun, sweetie. See you tomorrow."

I felt I had made a mistake about the dance. What an idiot—no one goes out alone. But since I'd bothered to look nice, I decided I might as well buy myself a ginger ale and stand around for as long as it took to drink it. Then I could leave.

I didn't have to stand at the edge of the floor too long before someone asked me to dance. It turned out to be that kind of function. Even people who had come with partners switched partners often; no one was jealous. There were plenty of smiles to go around. I was grateful for that. The band had a small horn section, and they played swingy versions of Christmas songs. Lots of people wore Santa hats. All the bins of records had been pushed to the edges of the room, and the drop-tile ceiling had been decorated with very used garlands and colored blinking lights. I danced with a lot of sweaty men, all of whom thanked me and declared me a good dancer. They seemed sincere, and I wanted to believe them.

At the end of the night as I walked to my car, I saw that most people had come in pairs or small groups. Now they laughed and chatted; someone imitated a trombone, and one couple polka-ed to their station wagon. A woman in a short red dress shouted, "There's Penny! Good-bye, Penny." I waved. Her husband had judged me the perfect size and had swung me over his head and under his legs. His wife was too tall for that, he'd said. "Thanks, Penny!" she shouted out the passenger window as her husband started the engine.

After the dance I pulled into a space in front of my building and admired the ice on the tree branches, glistening in the gold glow of the sodium vapor lamps. That beautiful, warm music played in my head, note for note. I didn't notice Clarence waiting by his truck, which was parked in front of my building. In fact, I would have walked past him had he not called out.

"Hey, Airhead!" he said.

I jumped.

"Jesus, Clarence, you scared me. What're you doing here?"

"Happy Thanksgiving to you, too," he said. He came over and wrapped his hand around my upper arm and bent to kiss my cheek. I winced.

"You reek of smoke," he said.

"I was at a dance."

"Who dances on Thanksgiving?"

"A lot of people. It was fun." I was looking down, hoping he'd let go of my arm. It would be pretty easy to bite him, I thought.

"Since when do you like to dance?"

"Since always. You're squeezing. It hurts."

He let go.

"Well, my parents were asking for you."

"That's nice."

"Aren't you going to ask if I had a good time?"

"Did you have a good time?"

"Not really. Not as much fun as you had."

"That's too bad." I imagined punching through his chest to his heart and my fist bursting through it, making it explode like a blown-up paper sack.

"Aren't you going to invite me in for some of that cake?"

"It's gone," I said. "I took it to work."

"You let a bunch of strangers eat it? That figures."

"I have to go to bed." I knew there was more to this conversation, and I didn't want to give Clarence the chance to get to his point.

Then he grabbed me by both arms. "I've been missing you," he said. "Haven't you been missing me?"

Clarence had always been unpredictably ardent. My resolve, such as it was, wavered.

"Maybe," I said, "a little." The truth was I hadn't been thinking about him much the last few days.

He pulled me close. I was still looking at the sidewalk. "Look at me," he said. He had that totally wounded look on his face, which seems to have a direct influence on the part of me that is all reaction and no sense. I let him kiss me, and how can I explain? It felt wrong but like a victory, too. Upstairs, in bed, I saw over Clarence's shoulder my new satin skirt draped over the rocker. I didn't shut my eyes all night. If Clarence noticed, he didn't say anything. He fell asleep around three in the morning and I stared past him out the window until it was time to get up.

As a joke the next morning Ren put on one of my nightgowns and cooked us breakfast. The pink satin gown was something his mother had given me two years before, and I'd saved it for sentimental reasons. I never wore it myself. It hit him mid-calf and looked repulsive. I don't think anyone would have looked good in it.

"Your place is a wreck," he said. He was lying on the bed watching me dress for work. "Where did you get that skirt?"

"I bought it." He was starting to get on my nerves. I stood in front of him with my hands on my hips. "I have to go soon. Why don't you get dressed?"

He didn't look directly at me. "I thought I'd stay here and clean up a little. I have to make a few phone calls, too."

He was trying to insinuate himself into my life again, like some kind of bacteria. If you don't take your antibiotics completely, the sickness comes back. Last night had been a mistake, and I was hoping he'd leave quietly and be gone when I came back from work, so I left him there in my pink satin nightgown.

At work, I had a hard time settling down. Most people were taking the holiday, so I stood in the kitchen a while, wasting time. I called home to see if Clarence was still there; the line was busy. Then I went through the refrigerator and threw out everything that looked old— baked beans with white fuzz; an open can of peaches, all but dissolved in their own juices; a Styrofoam carryout tray with the watery remains of a Mexican salad. When there was nothing left in the fridge, I went to answer some letters.

Dear Miss Straithorn:

No one's ever sent me flowers before. My wife got flowers, but never me. Please accept this gift in exchange.

Respectfully,
George Mobley

It was a country ham, wrapped in cloth and then in netting, and it must have weighed fifteen pounds. Handwritten instructions had been tied to the netting: "First, scrape away mold. Next, soak in lukewarm water for twelve hours."

I burst into tears like an idiot. What was I supposed to do with fifteen pounds of salt-cured ham?

"That's a nice ham," Gloria said mildly. She stood looking over the partition of my cubicle. "You make some nice hash with that. Put it on biscuits."

I cried harder.

When I got home at noon—Gloria had sent me home early—Ren was still there. He greeted me at the door with a slip of paper in his hand. I was cradling the ham in my arms like a baby.

"What's this?" Ren said, waving the sheet of paper. It was the guest list for my party. The one for which I needed to send invitations that very day, before it was too late.

"It's an invitation list," I said.

"'The Screamer'?" he read. "'The Nice Couple with the New Baby'? Are you sick? You can't invite people to a party when you don't know their names."

I snatched the list from him, awkwardly because of the ham, but he held on to the corner and it ripped. "I know them," I said. "They live next door."

"I notice I'm not on the list."

I hugged the ham close to my chest.

"That's because we're broken up," I said.

"Last night?" he asked.

"Mistake," I said.

Ren turned slightly, and the Christmas stocking I'd hung from the bookshelf caught his eye. It was mine from long ago, an old felt thing with my childhood nickname scrawled across the top in glue and glitter. How could I have let him see that? I was sure he would taunt me with the name, and the teasing would begin to feel like his thumb, pinning me in place. Instead of trying to get away, I would defend myself, and we'd start our thing all over again. He fingered the worn fabric, and I wanted to slap his hand away. He asked, very quietly, "Is there someone new?"

"For God's sake!" I shouted. "There's no one! I'm completely alone."

For a moment silence prevailed. Clarence looked sheepish, his face white and puffy. I thought of him, mere hours ago, playing the clown in my pink nightshirt. I felt the tiniest bit sorry for him. I wanted to throw the ham at his head, but the impulse led me to hold it even tighter. It was mine, after all—a gift—and I wasn't going to waste it on him.

Next door the New Baby started crying—a thin watery cry, which developed into a loud, insistent shrieking. The Screamer joined in, yelling unholy things about the New Baby and the other goddamn noisy neighbors. And couldn't anyone get some goddamn peace around here? The New Mother cooed anxiously to her New Baby. I would apologize later for my outburst, when I brought over their invitation.

"That skirt suits you," Clarence said, after a moment. "It looks good."

Boyfriends

When you die, your ex-boyfriends eulogize you.

Alberto Reyes takes the podium. Dogwood trees blossom behind him. As he speaks, the white petals drop to the ground.

"We square-danced," he said. "Her back was hot and her hands were cold."

Alberto is still twelve. He flushes red, and sweat breaks out along his hairline.

Gino Russo, who sat next to you on the bus, steps forward. He stands at the microphone and says nothing. His big brown eyes remind you of Sylvester Stallone's, and the horn of good luck glints around his neck. The two of you existed side by side on the green vinyl seat of the school bus, the wheels rolling beneath you. In the two days you dated during eighth grade neither of you said a word to the other.

Another quiet boy you'd almost forgotten nudges Gino aside. You never realized how many boyfriends you've had. This boy and his mother took you to a movie once. You debated the merits of the rock group Split Enz. He said he hated Bruce Springsteen. You stopped dating him after that. Now he says, "Springsteen is okay. *Ghost of Tom Joad* is his best work. Split Enz never got the credit it deserved."

You can't remember if Split Enz ever got the credit it deserved, and you're a bit peeved this boy hasn't said anything nice about you.

Max, the one high school boyfriend who made you melt, takes the podium wearing his blue uniform pants and blazer with the school crest. Underneath the blazer you know the sleeves of his white button-down shirt have been torn off. You also know that underneath his slacks, Max wears tight black bikini underwear. He grins.

"Mike and I, we were driving on the train tracks by Old Dixie High-way? Only the train started coming. So I said, 'Brace yourself, Mike. Don't lock your elbows.' Because then, you know, your bones will come right out of your shoulders."

This is Max's last story, the one he never got to tell. You are so mad at him. If you could speak you would say, "How dumb can you get? I used to dream about kissing you and wake up aching."

Post–high school: The College Boyfriend—the one you did wrong. The art student you cheated on with the business major. The art student wrote you postcards with hateful, gory poems. He reads one now:

> Your glass eye
> I hope it shatters

This stings, even though you don't have a glass eye. What a jerk, you think. Get over it. But then you remember how he used to bring you tea and muffins when you were studying, how he once stayed up all night typing one of your papers while you wrote another. Then you think of the business major in the chinos and pink button-down shirt, how he sweated beer the next morning and how repulsed you were. You can't explain to your art student why you did it, but you are sorry and you hate that he doesn't know.

Next comes your philosophy instructor, the seminarian who made you crazy by debating theology with you over the phone. He wasn't really a boyfriend, though he did kiss your cheek before going to Micronesia. You once lamented that you didn't feel you were doing any good on this earth, that maybe you should join the Peace Corps, become a social worker or a nurse. He said, "We need good people everywhere." You loved him for that. You can't wait to hear what he will say. He says, "The last step *is* a leap of faith. Try not to dwell on that."

Is it possible for the dead to be afflicted by stress headaches? You have one now, only this post-life variety is much worse than the kind you got when you were alive, the spasms that clamped down on your shoulders, turning your neck into a bundle of twisted metal cables. You try to calm yourself, but your eyes feel like hard-boiled eggs that have rolled back in your head.

Your first husband is here. He carries your small auburn-haired dog. He doesn't seem to realize that this is your funeral. As if at a mirror, he stands at the podium pursing his lips and pulling at the front locks of his hair. He checks his watch. You had accused him of being self-involved. He swore he didn't know what you meant. When you left, he said, "Why are you doing this to me?" You see now that he was too young; you were both too young.

A group of men approach the podium together. Their ages vary from early twenties to mid-forties. Some wear leather jackets, one wears a business suit, one running shorts and a singlet. They chat noisily, checking their watches as if making appointments to catch up with each other later, for lunch, racquetball, a jog. You wince, hoping that none of them will speak. These are the men you consorted with after your divorce: Ron the hairdresser, who gave you your post-divorce haircut; Paul the investor, who showed you how to get the most from your portfolio; Dean, the student who had no body hair. You wonder if Dean ever finished his master's, if Paul bought the boat he wanted. You wonder if any of them think of you. After this period in your life, you can no longer count on both hands the number of men you have slept with.

Your favorite husband emerges from the group of men at the podium. He looks older and even softer than when you first met. When you met—at your apartment, after it had been broken into—he sat at the table with you for hours taking notes on what had been stolen and what each item looked like. How long was the garnet necklace? What shape were the beads? What size? What a careful man, you thought. He filled out the paperwork, and when he wasn't asking questions directly related to the robbery, he asked about you. "You have a lot of books—you like to read? What's your favorite?"

On his way out he said, "Don't let this ruin your life." And he gave you his card. "Just in case," he said, "you notice something else missing."

Three days later, you called him. You wanted to tell him something else is missing, yes; could you help me find it? You set up a date. In a month you married this careful man.

Old habits die hard, and some of those men in the background weren't easy to let go of. You wonder what your favorite husband will say about this, your cheating, your "friends," as he called them. He adjusts his glasses, shuffles his papers, looks up.

"She was complicated," he says. "Too complicated for me."

He looks down as if to consult his notes, but then he folds them in half, turns, and disappears into the crowd of men.

Husband Number Three shows up—"the husband you truly deserve," as your best friend put it. Husband Number Three came ten years after your favorite. You had a successful career and no heart left to speak of, and the same was true for him. You were rich and shallow. So was he. You wish he wouldn't say anything.

"I bet you're glad about that pre-nup now, aren't you?" One of his children from a previous marriage stands with him. "Just kidding. Anyway, we had some fun, right?"

He holds up a curvy glass with a pink parasol crowning it. "Happy Trails," he says. "Send me a postcard."

Disappointment nearly swamps you, but you remember that this is the end of the line: You can't commit further transgressions, marry the wrong person, hurt people. Even though you are dead, this eulogizing has exhausted you, and you are ready for everything to be over—really over. You are about to sigh with relief and take whatever comes when your father appears at the podium. His eyes gleam with a fervor you've seen before: after the school play in which you played Antigone; the first time he walked you down the aisle. He carries a box that holds a gleaming white porcelain tea set nestled in dark pink tissue paper: a gift from your first and best admirer. As with so many things, this you have done nothing to deserve.

Do That Everywhere

In ninth grade, Cami Bradford quit band, dropped her AP classes, and started dressing differently from her twin, Kelli. She spent less time with Kelli and more time with Lynsey Budd, who said ninth grade was the year she would lose her virginity. Lynsey was dating a man who worked at Sound Advice Audio Salon on Route 9. He drove a Camaro and had a mustache. Cami had seen him pick Lynsey up from school, and she couldn't decide if Lynsey looked older sitting in the passenger seat of the Camaro or younger. The man's head, compared to Lynsey's, was huge. Cami liked the way he rested his hand on the back of the passenger seat while he drove, and she wondered what it would feel like to sit where Lynsey sat. The man had picked Lynsey up again today, so Cami walked home alone.

She pushed open the front door, dropped her book bag in the foyer. She heard the TV, so she knew Kelli was copying over her notes for AP English. They had been in class together until Cami had asked to transfer to regular English. Kelli sat on the floor at the coffee table, her three-ring binder in front of her. Oprah was on TV, and music leaked out of the headphones she wore.

"Hey," Kelli said. She was moving slightly from side to side, not in time with the music but in her own time. Wiggling, her mother called it—as in, "Stop wiggling, Kelli." Cami noticed the half-full glass of iced tea on the coffee table and knew Kelli was wigged out on caffeine.

In the kitchen, Cami took one of her father's copper beer mugs from the freezer. Her fingers left wet prints in the frost. She half-filled the mug with vanilla ice cream, then topped it off with root beer. She sucked the milky foam from the top and wondered what to wear to the party at Lynsey's tonight. Lynsey and Tabby Budd's parents were out of town, and the girls were having a welcome-home party for Trip Bannis, who was home—unexpectedly—from the military school he attended in Virginia. Cami had always liked Trip, and she wanted to look a certain way—older and pretty, though unconcerned with her looks, as if looking good came naturally. She scowled at her soda. From the pantry, she took a box of pirouette cookies.

Back in the den, in her father's big green recliner, she dipped cookies into her float and appraised her sister's outfit. The trick was suggesting that she not dress like a dork. Cami licked a glob of ice cream from the back of the spoon. She finished her soda by trying to suck it through the cookie, then abandoned the soggy cookie at the bottom of the mug.

"Let me fix your hair," she said. She had in mind exploiting her sister's cuteness, going for a wholesome-slut look.

Kelli nodded and wiggled a little more noticeably. Cami sat behind her on the couch and took up her sister's blond hair.

"Did Tabby Budd do your color?" Both girls had dark, satiny hair naturally. Their mother, also a brunette, couldn't understand their desire to be blond. Before the divorce, she often had tossed her sleek bob and reminded them that being a brunette hadn't kept her from getting a husband.

"Yes," Kelli said, "that bitch. She left it in way too long."

"It's not bad," Cami said, pulling her sister's hair into two sections. "It just doesn't have the same depth."

"That's what it is," Kelli agreed, nodding. "*You are so smart,*" she said, in her imitation grown-up voice.

"*Don't hide your light under a basket,*" Cami responded automatically in her guidance-counselor voice. Kelli snorted at this.

"Bitch Tabby asked me why you don't bleach your hair anymore."

Cami felt a grab of panic at her heart. "What did you say?"

"I told her you don't feel like it."

"What did she say?"

Kelli made a face and cocked her head to one side in imitation of Tabby Budd.

"*Obviously.* Then I made myself throw up on the rug."

This had been a trick of Kelli's since childhood: she could make herself vomit at will.

Cami finished the braids and went around front to look. "It's OK. Cute, but kind of dorkish."

Kelli touched the ends of her pigtails.

"Hance is coming over to help me with Bio," Cami said. "An experiment—with plants. When's Mom coming home? I need to go to the store for cups."

"*You forgot,*" Kelli said in her detective voice, her eyes narrowing, "*that Mother won't be home until tomorrow.*"

Cami imagined the reason for her mother's lengthened business trip: a brown-haired man who looked a lot like her father, who didn't dress as nicely and probably had bad breath. Her throat tightened, and she swallowed the burn, just to make sure she still could. "What am I supposed to do now?"

Her unlucky childhood trick had been, and remained, the ability to fall apart utterly at the snap of a finger, a word, or seemingly nothing at all. Sometimes this was intentional and sometimes not, but once she started she had little control over stopping. The full plate her mother had served her at dinner the day after her father left them—the green beans, the instant mashed potatoes with the puddle of margarine in the depressed center, the crusty meatloaf—had set her off and caused her mother to slam her own plate on the table, green beans flying, and scream, "What are *you* crying for?" Cami cried through dinner and dessert, through every forkful of food. "Well," her mother had noted, "I see your appetite hasn't been affected."

Kelli rubbed her sister's shoulder with the back of her hand. "Don't freak," she said. "We'll walk up to the Wa."

On the way, Cami told Kelli about the man who picked Lynsey up after school. "He looks old," Cami said, remembering the man's big hands on the steering wheel of the Camaro.

"Dad's age?" Kelli asked.

"Not that old," Cami said.

A man driving by in a red Z-28 yelled, "Sit on my face!" The girls ignored him, but Cami felt a quiver somewhere below her stomach. At the Wa they found the cups and had the cashier make them a cheese sub, which they split and ate as they walked home.

"Do you think they've done it already?" Kelli licked the mayo-mustard from the end of the sub.

"No. They're doing it tonight. Lynsey's calling me tomorrow morning to tell me about it."

"Can I listen?"

Cami shrugged. "Just don't laugh."

"You could do it," Kelli said. "With Hance."

"I don't want to," Cami lied, "with Hance or anyone."

"Why not?"

"You do it."

"No," Kelli said, shaking her head.

"*Why not?*" Cami said, in her Kelli voice.

Cami surveyed the yard where she'd arranged fifty plastic cups of soil and seeds, spaced far apart. Hance came through the back gate, picking his braces. He watched the cups as if waiting for the shoots to push through the moist soil and unfurl their leaves.

"Birds," he said, "will eat the seeds."

Cami ignored him. She fished in the pocket of her jumper for sunflower seeds. Hance walked over and helped himself to the seeds. She held perfectly still while he fumbled in her pocket. They sat on logs behind the compost heap. Cami's father had started composting the year they'd moved in, when the girls were three, intending to start a garden. Somehow the garden had never materialized, though the compost often sprouted miniature crops from the family's table scraps: squash, pumpkin, watermelon—all, at one time or another, grew here unbidden. Every once in a while Hance thrust his hand into the pocket of Cami's jumper for more seeds. Underneath her clothes, her skin felt prickly and hot, as if his hand burned her through the fabric. They spat the shells into the grass.

"Walk over to the party with me later," she said.

"Get Kelli to."

"She has too much homework," Cami said. They hadn't discussed it, but this was probably true.

"Trip got kicked out of school," Hance said.

This excited Cami, though she couldn't say why. She ducked her head so her hair covered her face and Hance wouldn't see her smile. Lately, her body reacted to things in a way she couldn't help or explain.

"He got some girl pregnant."

Cami felt suddenly foolish in her jumper.

"Maybe it was somebody else."

"He said it was him."

She wondered if Trip liked the girl. She wondered if Tabby knew.

"Who was the girl?"

"Nobody," Hance said.

"Oh," Cami said. The sun was setting, and the sky looked washed out, flushed of color, except for a few pale pink streaks.

"I have to get ready," Cami said, standing.

Hance followed her into the house. She went to the upstairs bathroom to clean up. After she got into the shower, the door opened. She heard Hance lift the toilet lid and unzip his fly.

"There's a bathroom downstairs," she said.

"I like this one," he said.

"Do you think it was on purpose?" she said. She sat on the floor of the shower, washing her hair.

"Was what on purpose, retard?"

"The baby. Maybe they wanted it."

"Trip's an ass," he said.

Cami lay on the floor of the shower. With her eyes closed tight, she massaged her scalp, letting the shampoo lather slide over her ears and down her neck. What if she opened the curtain and let Hance see her? He would say "What're you doing, retard?" and she would be forced to admit that she didn't know.

Once, when they were five or six, Hance had stepped behind the row of bushes at the front of the house, unzipped his fly, and whizzed against the foundation. Cami had followed the stream from where it started at Hance's small soft thing to where it darkened the concrete slab. She realized she should look away, so she pretended to examine the drainage pipe coming from the gutter. She thought how small and soft it looked—as if she could pinch it in half with just her two fingers—and she wondered what it looked like now. She heard him close the lid and run the tap.

"Adios," he said.

She rested her hands on her belly and thought of what Tabby Budd had said, that the space between a woman's hip bones should be hollowed out or at least flat, so when a man looks at a naked woman he would see that place as a cradle for his babies. Mine rises like a hill, Cami thought. She wondered if this was why her father had been attracted to her mother, who always looked slim in her silk kimonos. A month ago when she last saw him—backstage before his concert, wearing the dark purple jacket, smelling like limewater aftershave— he had made a comment about her size. He leaned in to kiss her, her good-looking, good-smelling, classical guitarist father, and said, "You're getting a little broad in the beam, aren't you, Dolly?" And her stomach had dropped and she had felt suddenly empty even though she and Mother and Kelli had just come from a big dinner at The Magic Pan.

"Play tennis with me Saturday?" he'd asked, and he'd given her arm a squeeze and smiled over his shoulder at his agent, who, Cami saw, had a very small waist and very large breasts. Her nipples poked at the black fabric of her tight sweater, and she bent slightly at her tiny waist and said, "Beautiful. Your daughter is so beautiful."

Cami didn't see how she could be beautiful when she didn't look anything like her father's agent. In the shower, she made fists and punched her thighs.

After dinner, Kelli and Cami cleaned the kitchen. Cami wanted to talk to her father, to hear his voice ask her about school and homework, to tell him she'd been playing guitar. She wanted to tell him about Trip and ask him what now would happen to that girl. She would tell him that Mother was gone on business, which would cause him to swear, and that there was a party tonight—that she was thinking of going. He would tell her certainly not, that his daughters didn't go to parties; his daughters stayed home nights and did their homework, even on Fridays. That would make missing the party all right—if he said she couldn't go.

"Do you have the number where Dad is?" Cami asked Kelli.

"You can't call him—it's Russia. He's with the oboe guy."

Cami felt tears collecting in her lower eyelids, but she ignored them and repeated half of what her mother would say—had she been there—in her best mother voice. "*That tour won't pay.*"

And Kelli finished it. "*The oboe should solo.*"

When they finished the dishes, Kelli mixed them both big glasses of Nestea, an extra scoop in each. The ice cracked and popped in the glasses. She thought if she could get Kelli to come to the party, they could always leave early. Everyone would understand that they were leaving because of Kelli, or at least with a roll of her eyes in Tabby Budd's direction, Cami could imply that. She surveyed her sister's velour sweats—indoor wear that predicted a cloistered weekend. She hadn't been wearing them very long. Maybe she could be persuaded.

"Tabby and Lynsey are having a party for Trip tonight. Come with?" Cami said. "We don't have to stay long."

"I have homework," Kelli said.

"Me too," Cami said, but the plant experiment was her only homework, and for now that was done. "You have all weekend."

Kelli hesitated, not because she was seriously considering the party, Cami knew, but because she hated to be pressed, and she was trying to think of a way to definitively refuse the invitation.

"Tabby thinks I'm sick." She scrunched her face up in an elaborate apology. "I don't like Trip," she said. Her face was now a deep shade of red, and a fine sweat had broken out on her nose. Cami smiled at this—her sister's one uncontrollable show of discomfort. Kelli twisted her face into another apology. "He smells weird."

Cami laughed. "I never noticed," she said, but she had. There was an oily smell, which she found exciting, overlaid with drugstore cologne that smelled like chemicals. It struck her as inferior to her father's. She thought someday of giving him something nicer-smelling, perhaps for Christmas. Such a gift would mean all sorts of things she couldn't name but could feel—in her chest, in her impatience with her sister.

"Please?" she said. She sidled up to Kelli, squeezing her arm and poking her in the side. "I'll do something nice for you."

Kelli squirmed away. "Check before you go. If I'm awake—maybe."

Cami took that as a likely 'no'. She went into the bedroom her parents used to share and took her father's best guitar from the closet, his five-thousand-dollar guitar, which her mother had insisted on taking from him. Cami played it every day, for at least fifteen minutes. She cleaned the strings after she played as she'd seen her father do, wiping them with a soft rag. She liked the smell of the guitar, and the way the last note resonated when she stopped playing.

Early on he'd given her lessons. Really, he'd just taught her to hold it properly so her wrist didn't twist awkwardly, so her hand cupped the neck in the most natural way. Then she had taught herself from books. Her father had liked the idea of an oboe and guitar duo, so she learned oboe too. They played together, and Cami thought he could tell she didn't like it and that was why they'd stopped. She'd quit band, there being no point anymore in pretending to like the oboe's nasal voice. He'd tried to teach Kelli, but the double reed proved too difficult for her, and she cried and cried until finally Mother said, "For God's sake, why can't you leave those girls alone?"

"Because that's all you do," he'd shouted, spit flying. "You do nothing but leave them alone."

There had been a big fight. Kelli and Cami sat on the logs behind the compost heap, smoking clove cigarettes Lynsey Budd had stolen from Tabby. Cami liked the sweetness—like dessert—and she licked it from her lips. They smoked and listened to the shouts of their parents, which sounded like the barking of dogs. The sun was setting, it was cold, and a white streak of jet exhaust dissipated in the sky above them. Their father had left that night, and for the rest of the week, Cami would sneak into her parents' bedroom, uncap the bottle of her father's limewater aftershave, and inhale. There was something missing in the smell, something from underneath the initial whiff that couldn't be gotten from the bottle. She went to the closet and found her father's tuxedo—the one he wore for special concerts. She crunched the white shirt in her hands and buried her face in it, breathing deeply. Here was the scent missing from the bottle. At the end of that week, her father had come to the house with his agent to get his things. "Your mother's not a bad person," he said, and then he left for good.

Kelli was asleep, facedown on her chemistry notebook at ten o'clock. Cami sighed, covered her with a blanket, and turned out the light. Back in her room, she dressed in a pair of tight dark jeans, a low-necked sweater, and black boots. She brushed her hair until it hung like satin sheets against her cheeks, then tucked it behind her ears. At her mother's vanity, she found a bottle of perfume and sprayed one wrist. She uncapped several lipsticks, searching for the right shade. All her mother's lipstick looked the same—reddish-brown—so she chose the one that appeared least used.

Outside, the moon showed high and clear, and the cool air stung her nostrils. Hance's house was diagonally across the backyards, and she scuffed through the leaves, around the compost heap—which had sprouted pumpkins and zucchini this year—and through the neighbors' yards. She stood under his open window and called to him. In a minute she saw his blond head at the window. Another minute and he was out the back door, wearing his sweats and sneakers.

"I was just about to go to bed. What's up?" He wouldn't look directly at her, she noticed, but off to his left instead, as if someone he really wanted to talk to was over there. That made her angry, and she automatically felt inclined to meanness.

"I'm going to the Budds'. Are you coming?"

"No," he said. "I'm tired."

Cami felt slighted. "Fine. Have a good sleep." She turned to walk away, but Hance grabbed her arm.

"Don't be all mad. And don't say you're not, 'cause I know you are."

Cami smiled but wouldn't look at him. She bit her lower lip and tried to pull away. He yanked her arm and put her in a headlock.

"You're messing up my hair," Cami said, struggling.

"*You're messing up my hair,*" Hance said. He released her. "When did you get to be such a girl?"

Cami laughed and tossed her hair. "You wouldn't know a real girl if you fell over one."

Hance charged at her, and she ran shrieking across the yard. He tackled her in the Eiglers' backyard, and before she hit the ground, Cami saw Mrs. Eigler in the kitchen window. Hance landed on top of her, knocking the wind out of her. He pushed her shoulders down, pinning her, and started counting. Cami lay there, paralyzed. She remembered her parents laughing once on the couch, when she and Kelli were younger. Cami's father held her mother's wrists and kissed and kissed her knees where the kimono had fallen away while she shrieked and laughed. Cami and Kelli had watched, giggling. She looked at Hance, who wasn't looking at her. She couldn't move. When he got to ten, he released her. "That was too easy," he said, rising. He turned to walk back to his house. "Have fun at the party."

Cami lay in the grass panting.

Mrs. Eigler called from the back porch. "Cami, is that you?"

Cami resisted the urge to say, "No, it's Kelli." She walked over.

"Hi, Mrs. E.," she said.

Unlike Cami's mother, Mrs. Eigler was stout—big around the middle after four boys. She had soft, pudgy hands, and Cami's mother enjoyed making fun of Mrs. Eigler's minivan and her pristine white running shoes. "That woman never runs anywhere, except to the fridge," she'd said once.

"What are you doing out so late?" Mrs. Eigler picked pieces of grass and leaves out of Cami's hair. "I love your new color," she said. "You look so much like your mom."

"Thanks," Cami said. "I'm going to watch movies with Lynsey."

"Ah," Mrs. Eigler said. "Let me give you some cookies to take over."

Cami's mother said Mrs. Eigler was disappointed because she'd had only boys. This was her explanation for all of Mrs. Eigler's kindnesses—they weren't because she liked Cami particularly, but because she wanted a daughter to mother.

Cami leaned on the kitchen counter, nibbling an oatmeal cookie while Mrs. Eigler packed a tin.

"How are your mom and dad?"

Cami shrugged. "Mom's out of town for work. Dad's dating some-one, and he's on tour in Russia." She shrugged again. "That's it, I guess."

Mrs. Eigler sighed. "Why don't you girls come for supper tomor-row? If I'd known you were alone I would've had you tonight. You can always come here, you know."

It shamed Cami that she felt more at home in Mrs. Eigler's kitchen than her own. That was her chief reason for avoiding it. At one time, she had hoped her father would date Mrs. Eigler, whose husband had died. She knew now this was foolish.

"Thank you. Thanks for the cookies."

Cami stared at the grass on the way to the Budds' and held the tin of cookies against her stomach. One of her parents' last fights—over a year ago—had to do, vaguely, with Mrs. Eigler. Cami's mother had made some nasty remark about Mrs. Eigler's looks—that she was frumpy, unattractive—and Cami's father had exploded: "She's twice the woman you are." Cami saw the disapproving look on his face, but her mother must have missed it because she smirked and said, "I'll say she is." Then Cami's father hurled the cup of tea he'd been hold-ing. The cup shattered against the wall, and Cami's mother flinched. Instead of screaming at her, the way Cami thought he would, he said quietly, "My god, Corinne, what has happened to you?" Cami stared at the shards of china. She felt sorry about the smashed rosebuds. She hated herself for crying about the cup.

When she arrived in the Budds' backyard, she thought at first there wasn't a party. She had expected to see people outside talking at the picnic table in the glow of tiki torches, grilling burgers, riding the tire swing. Then she saw the light glowing through the red fabric hanging in front of a basement window. If she listened carefully she could hear laughter and faint music. Votive candles lined the concrete steps leading to the basement door, and a piece of tie-dyed fabric—this one orange with a hot-pink sunburst—hung in its window. She looked down at the tin of cookies in her hand and left them on the picnic table. The smell of incense filled the stairwell. Bells tinkled as she opened the door.

"Welcome, welcome," she heard Tabby Budd say. Tabby looked so happy, her arms outstretched, sitting on the floor between Trip's legs. She had tied a triangular red scarf around her chest, and a big tassel dangled from its lowest point. The low-slung jeans she wore showed off the bell of her hips and the pale glow of her skin. When Tabby saw Cami, she dropped her arms and said, "Oh. It's you. Well, welcome anyway." She giggled and threw her arms out again.

In a gold velveteen chair, Lynsey sat on the lap of the man with the mustache. Cami thought his razor stubble made his face look dirty. One of his hands rested frankly between Lynsey's skinny legs; the other rested on her back, underneath her lavender sweater. She looked so small on his lap. While Cami watched, the man took Lynsey's face in one big hand and guided her mouth to his. He could eat her up, Cami thought. She imagined the man pushing Lynsey's head into his mouth. Lynsey and the man pulled apart, and Lynsey's lips shone with spit. Cami turned away. She felt as if she were underwater.

Trip got up to greet Cami. "Hey, Cami-girl." He enveloped her in a bear hug that almost knocked her backwards. He smelled of alcohol. When he pulled away he held her head in his hands and said, "You are such a sweet baby for coming." He kissed her forehead and left his lips there as if to rest himself. "Sweet."

Tabby stumbled over. "Where's your sister? Is she still sick?"

Cami remembered Kelli's throw-up scene and made a pouty face. "She said she's sorry she couldn't make it, but her stomach hurts from tossing."

Trip and Tabby made sympathetic cooing noises. Trip wobbled a little, then smiled and grabbed her arm. "C'mon, make you a drink."

Someone had hung paper lanterns in the den, and in the faint glow Cami could make out the forms of couples on the couch and the floor. In the kitchen, bottles populated the table and the countertops. Away from Tabby, Trip didn't seem so drunk. Beyond him, in the dining room, Cami saw the silhouette of a couple sitting on Mrs. Budd's mahogany table. They seemed to be eating something, but Cami couldn't be sure.

"You don't look like a baby anymore," Trip said. "How old are you?"

"What's it to you?" Cami dragged her gaze away from the couple on the table. She took the creamy drink he offered and sniffed.

"*What's it to you?*" he mimicked. "You're a fresh brat." He laughed. "That's Nuts and Berries."

"What's in it?"

He came around to her side of the counter and bent slightly to her ear as if telling a secret, kneading the back of her neck with his hand at the same time.

"Chambord," he murmured. "That's the raspberry."

"I like it," she said.

"All sweet girlies like it," he said.

She couldn't look at him, and she wondered if he meant to kiss her and if he could do that when she wouldn't meet his eye. He stood up straight and turned her away from him, rubbing her neck and shoulders as he pressed against her.

Cami let her breath out slowly and was surprised to hear herself say, "Mmmm." She licked the cream from her lips and felt the vapor of alcohol permeate the roof of her mouth and invade her nostrils. "What's the other taste?"

"Tastes," Trip said. "There's cream. You've had cream before, right?" He laughed softly and nipped at her neck. What he said sounded sexy and bad, but she didn't understand what he could mean by it. The tone of his voice seemed to wind its way inside her. "And Frangelico—that's hazelnut."

She knew she should say something, but she wasn't sure how this conversation was supposed to go, what the options might be, or even how she wanted it to go. "Does Tabby like this?" she asked.

Trip dropped his hands and sighed. "Tabby, Tabby, Tabby. She drinks everything. What else did we come for? Smokes for Tabby," he said, scooping up a pack of clove cigarettes.

On the way down, they passed two couples going up.

"You were gone too long," Tabby whined, pulling Trip onto the sofa. They were the last three in the basement, and Cami felt out of place. She stood in front of the sofa compulsively sipping her drink, wondering where Lynsey and the man had gone. Tabby and Trip stared at her from the couch as if she were a dumb TV show.

"You like him, don't you?" Tabby said, sounding flat and looking blank. "You think he's cute."

Cami imagined throwing her drink down and racing for the door. Trip laughed softly.

"She's damn cute," he said.

Tabby cocked her head. "She is a cute girl." Then she cupped her hands around Trip's ear and whispered something. Trip looked at her, then at Cami, and leaned forward, hand outstretched. He grabbed half of Cami's rear end and gripped her hard, pulling her to his open mouth. Cami was surprised to feel his damp breath through her jeans, right before he nipped at her crotch.

She yelped and swatted Trip's head. Her drink spilled over her hand as she twisted to get away. She backed toward the door. Tabby and Trip were laughing, Tabby with her eyes closed, leaning back, sliding off the couch. Trip said, "She told me to do it, Cami. She said you'd like it," and he reached out his hand to her. Cami walked out.

Realizing she still held her glass, she set it down on the top step. She was surprised how sharp his teeth had felt, and she couldn't understand why he would do that, or why Tabby would tell him to. She thought somehow it was flattering, but she also knew it was meanness on Tabby Budd's part. So lost in thought was she that she failed to notice the man Lynsey had been with. He sat on the picnic table by the tire swing, smoking a cigarette. The swing swayed slightly, as if someone had just left it. Cami noticed that the tin of cookies was gone. The man didn't seem to be waiting for anything. He looked at Cami a long time before speaking.

"What's up?" the man said.

"I spilled my drink," Cami said, shaking the last drops from her hand.

"Bad girl," he said. It sounded like a compliment.

"Where's Lynsey?" she asked.

"Fixing her hair," the man said.

Cami couldn't tell if he was serious. The man lifted his chin at her.

"You want a cigarette?"

"Yes, please." Cami walked over to the man and stood near his knees. He smelled of cigarettes and leather. She put the cigarette between her lips, and he lit it for her. She watched his hand with the silver lighter disappear into the front pocket of his jeans. How could it fit in there, Cami wondered. His pants were so tight. She caught herself looking at his crotch.

"How old are you?" the man said.

"I'm in Lynsey's grade," she said. "We walk to school together."

She felt she couldn't stand so near the man without trembling. She dropped her cigarette, ground it out more delicately than she normally would, and then sat in the tire swing. The rope squeaked against the groove it had worn in the bark. The man threw his cigarette in the grass and let it smolder there. He took her by the waist, pulled back, and let go. She twirled and spun, and her weight and momentum brought her back to him. He pushed her, and she went higher, spun faster. She shrieked and felt her stomach go light. The man kept pushing, and with every upward swing she felt lighter and lighter, until her insides—from her stomach through her chest—felt like a column of swirling air and mountainous churning clouds. She shrieked with laughter and finally gasped, "Stop, I'll jump!"

The man caught her in the swing and held on. He helped her out of the tire, holding her elbows as she staggered. Her hair was a mess, and she didn't care. When she looked up, she faced the man. Her hands rested on his chest, as if they belonged there. She felt warmth through his thin checked shirt, and hardness. She wanted to say something that would make the man stay.

"Come see our pumpkins!" she blurted, and she thought she recognized this voice from some other place.

She took the man's hand—it was big, as big as it had looked holding Lynsey's face—and led him through the backyards. All the lights were out at the Eiglers'. In her yard, at the compost heap, the pumpkins glowed soft orange on their dull green vines. Cami collapsed on the grass.

"Welcome!" she said. "Welcome to the pumpkin patch!"

She had pulled the man down with her, and now they both lay in the grass, gazing at the pumpkins. Cami hoped he would think she was drunk.

"Aren't they nice?" she said.

"The nicest I've ever seen," the man said.

The man pointed to another vine—one with long yellowish-orange flowers, which were closed now, in the darkness.

"Zucchini," Cami said. "Squash."

The man tapped her nose with his finger. "I know what zucchini is," he said, pretending to be offended. "I wasn't born yesterday, you know."

Cami giggled. "Obviously."

The man laughed and tapped Cami's nose again. He leaned over her, and as she watched, he pulled open one of the shriveled blossoms, stroking an exposed petal with his thumb. It was too late for zucchini; the warmth of early fall had coaxed the buds to bloom, but recent cold weather had halted their progress.

"You can eat the flowers, you know," she said, and she remembered the time, when her mother and father were still together, that they fried the blossoms in batter and hot oil. Cami and Kelli had been younger, just girls, really, and Cami had watched them come out of the fryer as if this were nothing unusual, to eat flowers for supper. Later, when she found this was not typical, she had thought of her parents as exotic, rare creatures.

"That I didn't know," the man said. "You've taught me something."

Cami felt a surge of happiness and pride. The man's body next to hers felt warm, real.

He picked the flower and twirled it between two fingers. Then he brought it to Cami's lips, tickling them with the edges of the petals. He drew his face close to hers, until the petals tickled his lips, too. Cami closed her eyes. She imagined the back door opening and her father calling her name, saying, *It's late, get in here.*

The man said, "Maybe I can teach you some things."

Cami squeezed her eyes shut tighter. The man kissed her neck while she lay beneath him, motionless. He paused and murmured in her ear, "How old are you, really?"

She had been holding her breath. She dug her fingers into the man's back. He rolled off her, propped himself on his elbow, and regarded her frankly.

"You have to ask for it," he said. "I won't do anything unless you ask, but you name it, and I'll do it."

Cami saw herself in bed alone that night, waking up the next morning to Kelli in her pajamas watching cartoons and eating cereal. If she didn't say something, the man would leave.

"Kiss me there," she said, pointing to her knee.

The man obliged.

"No," Cami said, "on the skin."

The man rolled up the leg of her jeans and brought his mouth to her knee. He gave her a soft, dry kiss, as if he were afraid she might bruise. She led him to the back porch and made him wait while she changed into one of her mother's kimonos. She removed her clothing but didn't look at herself in the mirror. The silk against her skin gave her the shivers. Kelli's door was still shut, and Cami paused by it to listen; when she heard nothing, she took the stairs in her bare feet.

On the porch, the man waited in her father's rocking chair. She could see his face when he smoked, barely illuminated by the cigarette's tip. She sat in her mother's wicker chair and let her hair cover her face so she wouldn't see him. She was sure she heard her heart pounding. One of the neighbors rattled a trash can lid. She clutched the arms of the chair. The man dropped his cigarette on the porch. Who was this person who wouldn't ask for an ashtray?

He stood before her now. She crossed her legs, and the kimono slid open to her hips. The man knelt. He placed his hand on her thigh, pressing his fingers into her flesh. He kissed her knee and rubbed his rough cheek across it. Cami imagined he tore her skin, leaving dark raspberry scratches. She felt as if she were melting and freezing at the same time. The scratches opened out, grew lush and red, poured warmth. She shivered. "Do that everywhere."

Tea Set

You would give anything now for your daughter to stop crying. The two of you sit in your husband's Town Car, parked in the garage, the genteel door chime sounding coolly amid your daughter's snuffling and sobbing. You don't think of turning the key to silence the Lincoln; your husband used to do most of the driving.

You have to stop crying, you say. Please stop crying.

Your daughter tries to stop. She holds her breath for a moment. A red flush blossoms on her cheeks. Then she bursts out again, as if the hurt is that fresh, that immediate.

I'll give you anything, you say. Anything. If you'll just stop crying.

Your daughter stops crying. The car falls silent. Even the Lincoln is in awe of your daughter's new power.

I want a tea set, she says.

You swallow. I'll get you one.

And you do. It's a white plastic tea set in an orange and yellow flowered box. You wonder—Is this a bribe? Am I a terrible mother?

After work, after school, when you pick your daughter up, you hand her the box.

I got you this, you say. You wanted it.

You are afraid of your daughter. You want her to stop crying—forever.

She regards the cellophane window of the box. She knows this is the best you can do.

Thank you, she says.

For a while the car is quiet. The leather smell, comforting. Your daughter asks why you like to have soup for lunch. She holds the box in her lap. You tell her you like soup. She asks, Why? Why do you like soup?

Buoyant

Elise couldn't help that pregnancy made her so buoyant and prone to drifting. They had been picnicking on the banks of the river, she, her husband, and their friends, and as she floated on her back in the cool spring-fed waters, the sun slicing through the branches of cypress and oak, their voices sloshed in her ears. Her husband's bass vibrated most prominently; he quoted baby books to their friend Jenna, who was single and wore a red two-piece. Jenna's laughter bubbled up at *hemorrhoids,* and it was hard for Elise to tell the exact flavor of mirth. Was it sympathetic: "Poor Louis, poor Elise?" Was it general tenderness for the indignities of the human condition? Elise detected a hint of pleasure—a grim "serves you right"—along with a dash of mocking and a ribbon of flirtation, of a purely biological type. Louis had gotten Elise pregnant; therefore he could likely impregnate Jenna. This angle would appeal to them both—a mini-celebration of virility and fecundity, though Jenna's fecundity was untested—another potential source of envy and competition.

Elise heard all this in her friend's laughter, so when she began to drift with the current, she let herself be carried away. In the water, she didn't feel so huge. Well, she felt huge, but not heavy. The protuberance of her belly button made a triumphant little hillock, which she could see if she tilted her head up out of the water. She wanted to stick a flag in it, and declare it hers, for it was hers. This was sovereignty, this floating in the river. "An island of me," she said. "Us. Sorry."

They would look for her in the wrong places—the bathroom, the snack bar, the bathroom again—and this pleased her. She had become, until this moment, quite predictable, though she hadn't set out to be so. Who does? News of her impending arrival had brought delightful visions of meandering from her current path, into fields unknown. She and the baby would be in charge of themselves. They would explore their new parcel of domesticity. She imagined lazy picnics of homemade bread, honey-butter, and limeade, and sunny expeditions on rolling hammocks of loblolly, live oak, and palmetto.

In between bouts of nausea and fatigue, she and Louis had purchased a clean, be-tiled ranch, in a subdivision of deciduous saplings, pristine asphalt drives, and taupe and gray siding in all directions. One day she wandered into the baby's room and found the crib, the changing table and dresser, a glider, a few tiny thick-paged books, and a slovenly pot-bellied bear slumped against the musical nightlight. A sea-green nursing blanket slung over the arm of the glider insinuated desert-like expanses of sleepless nights. Her eyes had glazed over.

Ahead, across the shimmering water, she saw a boat launch, and without thinking she pulled up beside it. A tall man in cutoffs greeted her.

"Hey, lady," he said.

"Hey," she said, clutching a rusty lash cleat. She peered behind the man and saw at the river landing families grilling their lunches, and children playing Frisbee. She imagined walking by them to the shuttle, cold river water streaming from her sagging swimsuit and monumental belly.

"You know where you're headed?" the man asked.

"I don't," she admitted. "And I don't want you telling me."

"You sure about that?"

He was shirtless and deeply tanned. To Elise, that was a badge, a testament to years lived in the sun, which counted for something. The tan came with deep lines, around which his skin seemed to hang. She let go of the lash cleat before she changed her mind. The man saluted her as she drifted downstream.

A snake streamed by, and turtles plopped into the water from their sunny resting places on logs. River grasses stroked the undersides of her thighs. Little fish bumped her calves and heels. Spoonbills plucked through the shallows, creating storms of white sand underwater. Elise stretched and wiggled her toes. Without people around, she felt strangely confident. She knew she would soon feel hungry, and that eventually the water would become too cool. But now the river opened into a large clearing, and the sun shone through even more brightly. The surface felt warmer, and beside her a thick silver fish jumped and wriggled in the air. "I know how you feel!" Elise said, and she settled in to enjoy the sun. Shutting her eyes, she admired the red, gold, and orange bursts.

She must have dozed, for the colors had gone cool—blue, green, and deep brown. When she opened her eyes she found herself in a narrower part of the river. Almost no light penetrated the thick canopy of leaves and vines. The water felt cooler, and the cold burned away her lassitude. She righted herself, treading water. Here the river sank underground, connecting to its icy aquifer. The current pulled her to the edge of its big lazy circle, and she bobbed pleasantly.

With each circling, however, the current drew her in tighter. The first few times she tried to swim out of it, she reached the whirlpool's outer edge before it drew her back to the center. She stared at the banks of the river, but couldn't penetrate the tangle of undergrowth and cypress knees. She turned her gaze to the dark of the river, and stared hard at the place where it submerged. She saw an opening beneath the water, a blue cave toward which the current urged her.

For a moment, she imagined Jenna and Louis reclining on the riverbank, laughing and chatting in the sun, Louis stealing a glance at Jenna's unseamed belly. They didn't know this place existed. What might she find: A limestone cavern of stalactites and trickling falls; schools of goggled-eyed electric-colored fish; light playing on the chalky walls; a rush of air and sound from the streaming aquifer? Later she and baby would page through books, and Elise would point to pictures of amazing creatures. She would tell baby, "You were there. We went together." She took a deep breath, rising out of the water, and plunged into the vortex. Moments later, like a cork, she popped up. As hard as she tried to swim toward the cave's entrance, eventually, against her will, she bobbed to the surface. Over and over, she dove and resurfaced, shaking the icy water from her head and gasping for breath.

Voices drifted to her from the bank. The tall man in cutoffs watched. Louis watched. Jenna and all their friends watched as Elise wiped the snot from her nose, took a deep breath, and plunged again and again, until all she could do was float on her back. The current spun her. She heard Louis say *emotional*. She wished the tall man in cutoffs would punch Louis in his face. They talked about ways of getting her out. Jenna with her arms crossed looked smart, ornamental, and utterly nonfunctional. Elise pictured Louis hauling her from the water, where she had been wonderfully, and was now cursedly, buoyant. He would wrap her in a towel, hand her a sandwich, and pack her into the car. He might ask her, in front of everyone, if she had to use the bathroom before they drove home.

"I don't want to be gotten," she yelled from the water. "I don't want to be had."

Jenna snorted. "Too late."

The man in cutoffs said, "She don't need fetching, do you, darlin'?"

She felt sick from the spinning, and she was cold.

"No," she said. "I'm doing something."

They wouldn't go away. They kept watching, which made the whole endeavor annoying in the extreme. After she rested, she would try again to get below the surface, down so deep none of them would find her, and she wouldn't hear their voices either.

If the Heart Is Lean

I counted the till for the second time. I was off twenty dollars. The last of the customers shrugged into their coats and headed for the door. Alice Flood, who had been a friend of my father's, stepped up to the bar.

"Don't go stealing now. I know how you young girls are."

"Ha," I said.

"You come by the party tomorrow. Bring those nice beans you make."

I'd thought about not going and then imagined Alice coming to my apartment the way she had many times these last few years. She'd show up at my door in a flowery dress and high heels. She'd look at me in my t-shirt and jeans and arch one brow at me. While I changed, she'd hum and straighten the living room. Because of Alice, I had attended every wedding, baby shower, bridal shower, and funeral in Cumberland since my father died.

I had liked to amuse Larry with stories from these parties. If it had been a bachelorette party, Larry had likely attended the male version. I'd come home to find him waiting outside my apartment, flipping through a sales circular and singing softly: "Oh, the married men. The ma-ah-arried men . . ." Other times, I'd open the door to his knock and he'd stand hand over heart, eyes wide, feigning heart failure over some stripper's act. My stories had begun to sound the same: the bride's skittishness over her decision to wed culminated in a public display of vomiting and staggering, or attempted but thwarted lechery. The male version Larry told precisely; the groom's skittishness had to do with the realization that he was never supposed to have sex with anyone but this one woman he'd chosen, and their nights tended to end in the grim neighborhood of unrelieved arousal. "They're so young and dumb," he'd murmur, unbuttoning his shirt in my bedroom, "they don't even know what to be scared of."

Alice touched the sleeve of my sweater. It was the pink cashmere Larry had given me. "Right nice," she said as she rubbed the soft fabric between her fingers. I yawned so suddenly I didn't have time to cover my mouth.

"Look lively now, youngster," she said.

"Why?" I said.

"Because you're not dead."

Now the till was thirty dollars off.

Alice sighed. "I know you and Larry were friends."

My face grew hot. Alice hummed softly. I set down the stack of bills and then picked it up again. "Think how his wife feels," she said.

I looked up to see her expression, but she was busy buttoning her coat. "All right," she said. "See you Saturday, girl."

I nodded. "See you." I left the till and the night's account unsettled in the safe.

On Route 68 on the way to the morgue, deer and deer parts spattered the road—typical for this time of year. I tried not to look when my headlights caught the twisted hindquarters or white underside of a tail on the shoulder. They bounded through the hills, driven by hormones or pheromones or the crisp fall air. They leapt onto the roadway, their strong hearts pounding in their mighty chests. I didn't wince anymore, not since I'd seen the dying doe in the median, struggling to gain her feet. Blood had foamed from her mouth and stained the white bib of her chest. I thought I should stop, but what could I have done for her?

I had already spoken with Budroe.

"I need to see his heart," I'd said. I thought if Larry's heart was covered in fat I'd know his death was plain misfortune or genetics or too many fried oysters. But if the heart was lean I'd know something else.

The heart was small, with brownish spots. I'd expected something heavier and harder to hold onto, something massive and covered in a yellow, choking fat. I touched it gently with my forefinger. "It's small."

"He wasn't a big person," Budroe said. "Don't drop it now."

"It's cold."

"That's what happens." He didn't know about me and Larry, so he was matter-of-fact.

I handed him the heart. I looked around for other evidence of Larry—his pants, his keys, his wedding ring—all the things I was used to seeing in my bedroom. I'd spent so much time gazing from my bed at his keys on my dresser or his pants draped over the back of my chair that when I thought of him those first few days after his death, that's mostly what I saw—his pants or his keys.

"What happens to it?"

"You don't want to know."

He pulled the latex gloves off my hands. "I know what you do want."

I had no idea what that could be.

"You want a ride in my new truck."

I looked down at my hands. "What else is there?"

"Hush," he said. "Put your coat on."

So far he hadn't asked why I'd been so interested in Larry's heart. I guessed that a lot of his friends had asked to see bodies since he'd started at the morgue. Maybe my request hadn't seemed strange. What I wanted to know was how does a forty-three-year-old man give himself a heart attack and die?

In the truck, Budroe turned on the radio and Brenda Lee's voice filled the cab, telling us about Christmas and all the feelings we would have then. Thanksgiving hadn't rolled around, and the brown leaves still clung to their branches. We drove along Route 68, the slick pavement sending up a dirty spray. In the woods, wisps of cottony mist had started to gather round the trunks of trees. The mist would make it impossible to see the deer bounding out of the woods. I knew Budroe was a fine driver—careful and alert. After high school, he worked as a tow-truck operator, and he let me ride with him for a few days after my father died. We drove all over Maryland, West Virginia, Pennsylvania. He'd go just about anywhere for people. It was common for him to work sixteen- or eighteen-hour days, rolling down dark highways to rescue the stranded, who weren't always as grateful or cooperative as you'd imagine. I used to think of him as a knight, the way he'd answer the dispatcher so positively—no trip too far, no call too late. After a year of this, he became an EMT. All his jobs seemed to me lonely and worse.

We passed the exit for the Moose Lodge, where Larry and I had met and where our dates usually began. He'd come around after dinner with his family and sit at the bar while I worked. When I wasn't serving customers, we'd talk—really, Larry talked; he'd tell stories from construction sites where he worked—and I listened and laughed. Later, after I shut down the bar, we'd go to my apartment. Larry taught me the shag, a harmless enough dance—easy to do, he said, if you were too drunk or uncoordinated to really dance. I liked to imagine that someday we'd twirl and swing that way in public, and all the people we knew would be there, smiling as they watched.

When the night was mild and too pleasant to stay indoors, we'd go to a spot on his property where he'd build a fire. We'd drink hot whiskey with sugar and lemon, and he'd cook for me—things I'd never eaten: hare or roasted oysters, large hot peppers stuffed with fennel and sausage. He had taught me to build a fire, and as I broke twigs and fed the flames, I'd challenge him to cook stranger and stranger dishes. We had been eating trout with ginger sauce when I issued the fried-ice-cream challenge. His face showed no reaction.

"Child's play," he said. I'd only heard of fried ice cream. The dish sounded preposterous to begin with and impossible over a campfire. I underestimated him, of course. Not only did he do it, but he made the ice cream himself, in what looked like an old wooden bucket.

"Bread," I said one night.

He snorted in disbelief. In two days we had hoecake, cooked in an iron skillet slathered with grease.

One particularly fine spring night, I'd been made reckless from too much whiskey or the freshness of the air. "Wedding cake," I said.

He kept eating. I'd expected a snort or some other dismissal. I fiddled with the fire.

"With butter-cream frosting. And strawberry filling between the layers."

After he finished his plate, he told me this story:

His parents' wedding was held in a Baptist church. The reception, on the grounds of the church, was by necessity dry. Larry's father and uncles made regular visits to the parking lot, to nip from the makeshift bar in the back of some uncle's Buick. As the brothers stumbled and cut up and grew florid in the face of flock and minister, Larry's mother became angrier and angrier. By the time cake-cutting rolled around, she was as red-faced as her groom, and about as likely to carve him up as she was to serve cake. She didn't bother with the knife. Instead, she dug her hands into her own wedding cake and turned on her husband with two fistfuls of Lady Baltimore. The fluffy white frosting and delicate cake oozed between her fingers, and she smashed the mess of it in his face. Drunk as he was, he fell right over. "So the story goes," Larry said. I wasn't mad at him for refusing my challenge, though I believe he could have made a wedding cake over fire, if he'd really set his mind to it.

Budroe had been speaking. Elvis was on the radio, singing about Christ our savior being born, and he had called for a change of music. I don't know how many times he asked before I responded. He favored CCR, loud, so I set about looking for that.

"Your truck's disgusting. How can you find anything?"

"You sound like Cassie."

"I guess you better clean your truck then."

"I want you to do something for me," he said.

I wondered what he thought I could do for him. I stopped shuffling through a stack of CDs to face him.

"Keep an eye on Cassie tomorrow."

I stared at him. "The bachelorette party? At Alice's? I can tell you right now—nothing will happen." Alice would serve cake in her flowery living room and Cassie would open presents. We would watch and exclaim over the tacky lingerie she pulled from the boxes.

He took his eyes from the road to look me in the face. "Seriously. I don't want her getting sick or hurt. I know how stupid you girls get."

My head swam. "You got it." I slid a CD in and changed the subject. "I don't know why they don't *do* something about the deer."

Budroe took his hands off the wheel to count on his fingers. "We hunt. We hit them with cars."

"That's what I mean. It's gruesome."

"It's tasty, venison."

"You like it because it's what you've got. Why not put up fences?"

Budroe shook his head. "You can't stop this."

We passed another hunk of deer on the shoulder.

"Jesus," I said. "It's awful."

"It's life, darlin'."

"Getting creamed by a car is not a natural part of life."

I turned to put the rest of the CDs in the back and saw a metallic glint against the dark fabric of the interior. It was a very delicate gold hoop earring. I imagined the wisps of Cassie's long brown hair around it, and my face burned. I started to settle back in my seat and thought, "Oh, what the hell." Reaching behind again, I took up the gold hoop.

"You've got nice taste in jewelry." I held the earring up in the space between us. "Maybe if you work real hard at the morgue you could afford to buy the other one."

Budroe glanced at the earring and broke into the sweetest grin. I yawned in his face.

"It's kind of hot in here." I could hardly keep my eyes open. I put the earring in the ashtray. Slumped in my seat, I closed my eyes, cracked the window, and waited for Budroe to tell me the story of Cassie. What was it about her—aside from her beauty—that told Budroe he should marry her? What did he and Cassie do together? What did people who were about to be married *do*?

Instead of starting the story, he slowed the truck and guided it to the side of the road. I opened my eyes to flashing lights. Mist had collected at this low point in the road, and the glare from the red and blue lights on the wet pavement made it difficult to see. Budroe was already out the door, striding over to the scene. A white van rested on its side in the sheltering V made by two squad cars. Something lay in the road, and two EMTs walked quickly to it with a stretcher. My head felt suddenly light, as if it might float away. The EMTs rolled a deer onto the stretcher. Budroe talked with them a moment. What would they do with the deer? Could they really save it? Would they take it to animal rescue? Back in the truck, Budroe looked at me.

"You don't look so good."

"What about the deer?"

"He probably swerved to miss one, but who knows where it is now. One-car accident—what a way to go."

Budroe followed the ambulance to the emergency room, an ugly bright place. The people waiting for care looked pale and timid. No one cried or wailed, and I didn't see a spot of blood on any of them. In fact, everyone sat eerily still, as if resigned to, and grateful for, a long wait. As long as they waited, no one could declare them terminal, dead, infected, or anything. They could tell themselves whatever stories they wanted about their condition and believe them: the stabbing pain in the abdomen *was* gas; the blow had been *unintentional; everyone*, now and then, had back-wrenching spells of vomiting. I followed Budroe past the waiting area, and I stared at them. None made eye contact, as if willing themselves invisible.

We entered the ICU. The man-not-deer was dead, and we learned that the young nurse on duty who was to prepare his body for the morgue had been a high-school classmate of his. She sat beside the body.

"We used to say hey," she said. "We flirted."

"He's lucky to have you here," Budroe said.

The dead man didn't seem lucky to me. The nurse rose, and without a word she and Budroe began to work. They wiped the crusted blood from his ears and the fluids that had come from his nose and mouth. They cut away his clothes, shifting him slightly now and then, peeling away the fabric until he emerged in all his paleness. They tied his hands in front of him, and then they tied his ankles. He looked too small to be real.

Budroe was nudging my shoulder. "Wakie-wakie."

We were still in the ICU, and I was sweating inside my coat. The nurse was there, too. I thought she would tell me why I kept yawning and falling asleep all the time, or that I needed to be admitted for tests, but she didn't say anything.

"Are we going to the morgue?" I asked.

"We're all done," he said. They had left me sleeping and had already taken the body downstairs. In the hallway, after the nurse and Budroe said their good-byes, I took hold of his arm.

"I need to see him," I whispered. "*All* of him."

Budroe gave me a look that told me I'd gone too far. He started to speak a couple of times and stopped himself. Finally he said, "I can't help you there."

"I've already seen his heart. What difference does it make?"

"It's not him."

I thought I understood what he meant—that it was just Larry's shell, and what I knew of him was gone to me forever. I nodded and said, "I know that—"

"It wasn't *his* heart, is what I'm telling you. It was somebody else's. We keep it to show the high-school kids who think they want to be doctors."

I dropped my hand from his arm. "Oh," I said. I thought about how I would tell it to Larry. "All that time I thought it was *your* heart." That would be the punch line. "You thought that small thing was mine?" he'd say. "Don't insult me."

Budroe shook his head. "I thought it would help. Denise had him laid out in South Carolina. They buried him yesterday. Alice was supposed to tell you."

Budroe wouldn't let me drive. I made him take me to Larry's. I'm not sure why he did. We crossed the bridge over the tiny creek that separated Larry's land from the main road. A sign by the side of the drive read "For Sale."

"It's a real shame," he said.

I thought it was a shame—for me—but I was pretty sure he wasn't thinking that.

"Everybody—we just assumed you'd go to college. Then Larry turned up and it was like you were glued to the floor. We didn't know what to say."

I let that one go. It wasn't anyone's business. I could have snorted and said, quite rightly, that Budroe often didn't know what to say. Instead, I said, "I guess Denise is getting on with things," referring to the For Sale sign.

"Not really." I could hear the disapproval in his voice. "The bank is selling the house. Larry's construction business went under right before he died."

I was still wearing the sweater he had given me. I fingered the hem and thought of his kids having to pack their toys and move from their home in the woods to some small apartment in town. They'd be squeezed among other apartment houses and bars and small storefronts with pegboard displays in their windows. Mornings when they waited for the school bus, everyone who saw them would shake their heads.

Budroe parked in front of the house. Lights were on inside. I saw towers of boxes and Denise moving among them. "We thought you were smart and you'd be OK. Someone would have given you a scholarship."

"I wish you'd shut up about that." I watched Denise. "Or go to college yourself if you care so much, you hick."

Budroe's second-grade picture flashed before me. What sweet kids we'd been.

"Don't be a bitch," he said, a request.

"I'll be what I want," I said, the sad truth.

He inhaled deeply then sighed. "What you want to do?"

I half-shrugged.

"Want me to take you home?"

I thought about returning to the apartment. I would go to bed and wake up feeling better, though nothing would have changed. I put my hand on the door handle. "Leave me here."

"What for?" A light flicked on in the foyer of Larry's house. The front door opened, and Denise stepped into the shadows of the porch.

"Porch light's out," Budroe said. Larry had built the porch high. I imagined its rafters would make a good home for bats.

"You'd better talk to her. She sees your truck."

He nodded, and I slipped into the woods. It didn't take me long to get the fire going. For November, the night was mild. The smell of the woodsmoke comforted me. I sat on a log and gazed into the flames.

"Here's the story," I said. Larry would never begin in such an obvious way. "You're alive, and I'm dead."

I imagined Larry snorting at me for getting it wrong. On our last night together, I had been sitting up in bed scraping candle wax from my nightstand. He got up to use the shower.

"How did you and Denise meet?" I asked.

He paused at the bathroom door before entering. After the shower started, I went in and sat on the toilet.

"I'm gonna guess, OK?" He was washing his face—I could tell by the sound. Maybe he couldn't hear me. "You met at a bar. You told stories that *amazed* her and made her laugh. She couldn't resist you." I expected him to ignore me. From the shower, he said, "Our mothers were friends. That's how we met."

He didn't say anything more until he got out of the shower. He toweled off. "My mother was afraid I'd drink myself to death. Denise's mother was afraid she'd marry some bum she went to high school with. I don't know who got the worse end of it."

"You're not a bum."

"Thank you." He stood in front of the mirror combing his hair.

"You're not a dead drunk."

He bowed in my direction. "I thank you again."

I felt I should tell him something about myself, since he'd been so forthcoming. "My parents never married."

"Everyone knows that." He was still looking in the mirror, fiddling with his hair. "Tell me something I don't know, sweet thing."

My mind was a swirling vacuum of emptiness. I took up his hand, which was warm—rough and dry. "I could read your fortune in the palm of your hand."

He snorted. "Don't insult my intelligence."

I had to laugh. He made his way toward the fire escape. "Let's sit outside. Bring some beers." He still wore my pink towel around his waist.

We sat outside, dangling our legs over the edge. I was wrapped in a sheet. Anyone walking by would have seen us.

"Well, let's go. *Amaze* me."

I had only one story that no one else knew, and I told it to Larry then:

Every year on the Fourth of July, my father took me to the picnic his boss threw. When I was eight, we went as usual and Daddy turned me loose with the other children. I was getting a soda from the big aluminum tub, and this man I'd never seen before opened the bottle for me. He wore a cream-colored suit, and his hair was slick and blond under his straw hat. His shoes were two-tone—tan and cream. I thought he was handsome, like an actor from an old movie. He offered me his hand, and I took it. We got into his car, and I drank my orange soda as he drove away. The sun blazed through the windshield, and the leather seats felt slippery and warm under my cotton sundress. My feet didn't touch the floor. He winked at me, and I swung my legs. After about five minutes, he stopped the car and walked to the side of the road, disappearing behind the thick tangle of bushes and trees. I waited a long time for him to come back. I thought Daddy might have noticed I was gone, so I got out of the car and cut through the woods back to the picnic. I planned to check in with my father, then go back to find the man. I'd been gone thirty or forty minutes, and people had thought I'd wandered off and gotten lost in the woods. My father's face looked gray and twitchy. He scolded me lightly, not severely enough to anger me. I never saw the man again, and I never told anyone about him.

Over the years I'd imagined the man would have driven me down South, to Jacksonville, over the St. Johns River, where we'd had our family vacations. I saw myself as a woman on the beach, my hair blowing, my husband and children playing in the sand behind me. As I sat with Larry that night and gazed across the street at the highway overpass, I felt embarrassed by the memory. Cumberland was far from the beach, and I hadn't set foot outside it in three years. "Where do you think I'd be now," I said to Larry, "if I'd stayed in that car?"

He drank some of his beer before answering. "You'd be a pile of broken bones in a hole somewhere, love."

I decided not to tell him the rest of it, which was this: The memory I most cherished from that incident was the image of my younger self, slipping out of the car and into the woods. That girl knew exactly where she was; she wasn't lost, and she wasn't afraid. No one else had any idea where she was, but she knew—how to get home, how to get to the creek, how to move among any number of childhood hangouts. She was not lost.

I liked to imagine he would have been kind then, if I'd told him. "Of course you weren't *lost*," he might have said. "Just because *they* couldn't find you."

I waited most of the night for the fire to burn out. Budroe had pulled onto the shoulder of the road in front of Larry's and slept in his truck, waiting for me. He drove me home and didn't ask any questions.

If only out of habit, I got ready to go to Alice's party. She had taught me these last few years never to refuse an invitation if it was humanly possible to attend and never to say you're coming and not show. On top of that, I'd promised Budroe I'd look after Cassie, who didn't need looking after.

I waited a long time on the couch with my baked beans for Alice to fetch me. After a while I realized it would be strange for her to fetch a guest for her own party. Hadn't she said just to come? So I walked over with my beans. I hadn't thought who might be there—the usual crowd, I supposed. I rang the bell and Alice met me.

"Oh, darlin." I didn't like the look on her face. "You look right nice." She sounded almost sad.

"For a change," I said, finishing her thought. I wore a skirt she had given me last spring. Larry had said the large hibiscus pattern made me look like a beach umbrella.

"You brought your beans, I see," Alice said.

I moved to step into the house, but she blocked the doorway.

"Can't I come in?" I thought I was making a joke.

She rocked on her heels and said, very gently, "No can do, my sweet. Larry's widow is here."

Something swift and animal-like filled my chest. I wanted to run. "Oh," was all I could say.

Alice set her gaze on me and didn't blink. "Can't upset the widow, now, can we?"

I wanted to cry to Larry—something about the unfairness of it all—but it wouldn't do any good if I could have. He'd let me cry, and I'd know I was a fool to expect anything more.

"How *dare* you?" I choked out this much. "Who do you think I am?"

Alice frowned at my mistake. "Oh, dear," she said.

From the highway, a thread of tinny, jagged music wound its way through the breeze. The traffic on the overpass whooshed and thrummed. I saw Alice in her flowery dresses, straightening up my apartment and parading me around town for everyone to see. At best, maybe they thought I was a nice girl who got on the wrong track after her daddy died. I couldn't stand that. Alice opened her mouth to speak. I turned to go. It was my story, and I wouldn't let another tell it.

Embankment

After the man lets you out of his car along State Road 537, you stand
on the shoulder, in the darkness, miles from your apartment at the
shore. It's difficult to imagine returning to the place you share with
your sorority sisters, all of you part of a glut of pretty new would-be
teachers who have flooded the ranks of retail in 1970. You shift your
weight from one foot to the other, your hand on the shoulder strap of
your purse. What if he comes back? What if he doesn't come back?
You walk quickly down the road, your pantyhose scritch-scritching,
the lining of your wool dress shushing.

You see the headlights coming from behind and you veer off the
road, stumbling toward the woods. Your ankle turns and you fall to
the grass below the shoulder. Above you, the car has stopped and
you hear the man rustling around, fishing in his trunk for something.
You right yourself, placing your hand in a patch of wet leaves, and
wonder what your roommates are doing. You imagine them in post-
work mode: in bathrobes, their hair in fat plastic rollers, watching the
news or *Laugh-In,* Nancy filing her nails, Pam smoking, wondering
aloud where you are. "She's always getting *lost.*" Nancy defending you:
"Maybe she's at the store—buying ice cream." Little bits of decayed
leaves stick to your palm.

The man up on the road swings a flashlight. He is looking for you.
Your ankle throbs. Wiping your hand on your thigh, you regard the

sleeve of your overcoat—the camel-hair coat you've had since college. Your mother offered to buy you a new one when you graduated, and you thought, why? Soon you would have a new life, consisting of what you weren't sure, but you were certain you would become a different person, one who would need entirely different things. So you declined the offer of the new coat, because how could you foresee who you would become? You smiled at your mother, at her old lady hair. How could you explain? She had always known what she would be.

You flirted with the men who came into the shoe department at Steinbach's, even the ones with their wives. Joan, your supervisor, had once stroked your cheek with the back of her hand and murmured, "Sweet baby, this isn't a cocktail party." You blushed. Joan was pickled, your mother said. You had a sense of yourself in that gray-carpeted department, as something ornamental in your pink sweaters. Of the three of you, you seemed most destined for something meaningful and impressive. Nancy was too spacey and gentle, and Pam—a laugh riot—too abrasive. "Cultivate a low tone," you murmur—a piece of advice your mother had given you.

You recognized this man from somewhere, smiled when he approached you in the store parking lot. Dimly you placed him on your parents' back porch for cocktails, middle-aged and sweatered, a less fortunate business associate of your father's. He looked soft, possibly kind—the sort of man known around the office for making jokes, wearing strong cologne, and trying too hard. He mistakenly called you Cynthia as he took your arm and led you to his car. You laughed. "Am I being whisked away?" and you thought of Audrey Hepburn and Leslie Caron —another wisp of a girl danced away from her humdrum existence by some unlikely man.

He mistakenly called you Cynthia, and you corrected him in the car, the heater blasting against your knees. A squashed cup rested on the floorboard. The car smelled of cologne and something else you couldn't identify immediately. You frowned at a crumpled straw wrapper on the dashboard. Toothpaste? Bleach? Cleanser.

"Look, Cynthia," the man said, "I have a son who would love to meet you. He'd be so jealous right now."

You stared at the straw wrapper. You suggested that you might be tired, that you might go home instead of whatever he had planned for you.

He looked genuinely hurt and puzzled. "I'm taking you out to meet some people. I thought it would be nice." You tried to imagine having drinks with this short, curly-haired, possibly Jewish or Italian man. And here you became confused because he said, "I talked to your mother the other day. She's worried about your finding a husband." You looked at him sharply, and he nodded. This sounded like something your mother would say. Had you agreed to see this man? Consented to some plan of hers to meet a business associate of your father's in the store parking lot after work for drinks? Hadn't he known your name— almost? But why the hurried push into the car, as if he were shoplifting something he wouldn't even be allowed to buy? You couldn't think clearly in the car with him. It was possible your mother had arranged all this, and in your daze, your perpetual daze, you had forgotten. So you smiled and said, "Where are we going?" and you hoped it would be Georgia Brown's or someplace like that—dark and smelling of overcoats and hats. Or maybe he would take you to the shore, to the Stone Pony, but this seemed too young for him, and wrong for you, for someone serious, who wants serious things from life. So you asked the man, "Where to?" and he became angry. He pulled over. "This is wrong," he said, gripping the steering wheel. "What kind of girl gets into a strange man's car?"

"You said you knew my mother—"

He spoke patiently, quietly. "I think you'd better get out." And he put you out on the side of SR 537. You fell down the embankment, and here you are, damp and cold, your ankle swollen inside your pantyhose. You remember the feeling of a ligament tear from cheerleading and all the attention that came afterwards: the visits from joking friends and the squadron of ill-at-ease jocks making their duty call, how they'd horsed around on your crutches, large and vulgar in your room of girl things. So much attention had been paid you—a disgusting, embarrassing amount, your whole life—but it glanced off you. The awards, the praise of your parents, the celebrations with bakery cakes— you passed through these events, looking ahead to something foggy but glaringly bright.

The man calls your name and sounds fatherly—concerned, but also impatient. As in, I'm worried about you, Claudia, but if you don't answer this minute (young lady), I'm going to be very angry. You feel like a naughty, foolish child. If you move, he'll hear you, and you can't move much anyway. If you stay put, maybe he won't find you, though your coat will be bright in the beam of his flashlight. Your face grows hot. You hear yourself telling Nancy and Pam later how you evaded this would-be rapist, or business associate of your father's—whoever he is—by remaining perfectly still. Pam would say, "You should have let him take you out, Claudia." Nancy would smile gently. "You must have been so scared, Claude. Make you some hot chocolate?"

Your nose is running, and without thinking you reach for your purse and the pink tissues inside that smell of your Jean Naté cologne. The run in the knee of your hose annoys you: to spend what little money you earn on these things. Too, the snag implies something wrong about you. You feel sullied by it, and this annoys you more than having to replace them. You should keep an extra pair in your purse, and you blow your nose at the bottom of the embankment and think about what your mother said, that young women are often judged by the company they keep, and you wonder what this means for you. How do men judge you, in the presence of gentle Nancy and brash Pam?

You are something in between, something airy and bright, placid and reflecting, like the glassy lake in the Poconos where your parents took you skiing in high school. The lake before freezing, before the initial scum of ice, blazed with light. It was almost blinding. Your ski instructor, who was hardly older than you, noticed your squinting. "Snowblind," he said, and you squinted at his tanned face, admiring the fringe of blond hair around the edge of his cap. You knew everything: that you would sneak away from your parents that night and be with this boy. Your foresight startled you. But why? You were made for this, and so was he. You met every morning for breakfast, skied the slopes, met every night after dinner, even did it in the snow. You imagined your heat melting the snow around your bodies, and the melting would continue; in the morning everyone would wonder, what happened to all the snow? You and the boy would be gone—where? Here your imagination failed you. When you said good-bye in his cabin, his things scattered around the room somehow diminished him, especially his white briefs.

Riding home with your parents that morning, satisfied, you dozed in the back of the car in the warm sun like a cat. Two weeks later, nothing about your life had changed. You chafed at the supper-table conversation with your parents. At dances, you stared over the shoulder of your partner, impatient for something to materialize.

Then the teaching college for women. You groan. A mistake, you see now, and you've never felt more hard and more focused—not a fuzzy light, but a sharp beam. And it falls on you. You blink.

"Claudia," the man says.

"I'm here," you say, rising on your one good leg to meet him. You brush the leaves from the back of your thighs. "I'm here."

Acknowledgments

Thanks to the editors who published stories from this collection, in one form or another: Rob Spillman, *Tin House*, "Pretty"; Lynn Tillman, *FENCE*, "Mrs. Fargo"; Elisa Maranzana, *Hogtown Creek Review*, "Do That Everywhere"; Jeff Johnson, *JANE*, "Chestnut Season"; Mary Sue Koeppel, *Kalliope*, "Tea Set"; Sacha Feinstein, *Brilliant Corners*, "What Nina Wants"; Bill Henderson, *Pushcart XXVIII*, "Pretty"; Chris Bundy, *New South*, "Buoyant."

Thanks to Maggie Roche, for permission to use lyrics from her song "The Married Men."

For financial support, thanks to Miami University and The Ohio Arts Council.

Many thanks to Michael Griffith, Yellow Shoe series editor, for liking this book, and to the good people at LSU Press for all their work on its behalf.

Heartfelt thanks to the following for support, encouragement, advice, tutelage, mentorship, wake-up calls, and shoulders to cry on: Josh Russell, Padgett Powell, Nancy Reisman, David Leavitt, Brandy Kershner, William Logan, Debora Greger, David O'Gorman, Mark Devish, Michelle Gould, Bill Stephenson, Christina Carlton, Ashley Clifton, Ryan Meany, Joe and Gay Haldeman, Charlie Geer, Chris Merkner, Imad Rahman, Chris Bachelder, John Elderkin, Emily Miller, Tanya

Zarlengo, Martha Otis, John Morogiello, Paul May, Greg May, Cathy Fink, Marcy Marxer, Nicola Mason, Brock Clarke, Trent Stewart, Larisa Breton, Kaara Peterson, Brian Roley, and my wonderful colleagues at Santa Fe Community College and Miami University.

Thanks to Keith Tuma and my creative writing colleagues for taking a chance on me.

Thanks especially to my family, for the long-distance love.

Biggest thanks of all to Billy Simms, for believing in me from the start.